A THEFT MOST FOWL:

A KINGDOM OF AVES MYSTERY

NICOLE GIVENS KURTZ

MOCHA MEMOIRS PRESS

Published by Mocha Memoirs Press, LLC

ISBN: 978-1-7352195-7-8

CREDITS:

Cover art: Maya Preisler
Editor: Maya Preisler
Proofreader: Melissa Gilbert
Formatting: Kenesha Williams
Map of Aves: Sarah Macklin

For Weston

PATRONS!

Thank you, patrons, for continuing to donate and support Nicole's creative efforts and works.

- Aiesha Little
- Alledria Hurt
- Andrea Judy
- Bishop O'Connell
- Darrell Grizzle
- Joel McCrory
- Kenesha Williams
- Maya Preisler
- Paige L. Christie
- Patrick Dugan
- Rebekah Hamrick
- Rick Smathers
- Rie Sheridan Rose
- Samantha Bryant
- Allie Charlesworth
- Dino Hicks
- Michael Williams

You can join these wonderful patrons and support Nicole's work via **Patreon**.
Go here (https://www.patreon.com/user?u=19915635) to sign up.

ACKNOWLEDGMENTS

I would like to acknowledge the assistance and support of the following individuals.

Thank you to these amazing beta readers:

Susan Ragsdale
Becky Kyle
Dahlia Rose
Paige Christie

OTHER NICOLE GIVENS KURTZ'S TITLES

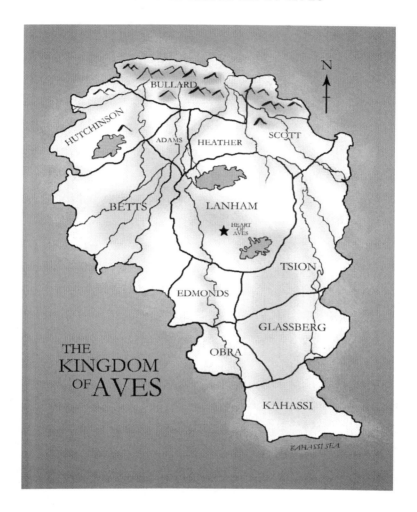

THE THEFT

The foggy night unfolded in hushed quiet at the University of Sulidae's Museum of the Goddess. A figure stepped out of the darkness, cloaked in the shadows filling the museum floor. Outside, the evening's cloud cover cast the entranceway in pitch-blackness so complete the campus lanterns struggled to penetrate the gloom. The darkness made it easier to hide. Achiel, *one*, had been given a new name, a secret one, blessed by the goddess. Using the museum's lowered lights, Achiel eased themselves from their hiding spot in the exposed ceiling beams. Security guards walked the floors every thirty minutes, and while they casually scanned the exhibit floor, they never looked *up*.

Achiel remembered the moment the goddess spoke to them. The powerful rays slammed into their skull. *I heard this huge crack, and it was my head.* The goddess spoke then and demanded their service. At last, their unique skills would be utilized for divine intervention. An exhilarating rush spread through Achiel as they conjured the magic from within their core and whispered, *"Levitate."*

The air lifted them into its embrace, and as Achiel spun their fingers around, they whirled softly before being placed on the floor.

Both guards stood talking together at the front entrance. Tiptoeing through the darkened pedestals and curtained exhibits, Achiel paused to review the signature pieces. They slipped between raised short walls and elegantly lit pottery. All of these beauties being locked behind protective glass evoked anger.

Soon, they will be returned to the goddess once more.

In their early youth, Achiel realized a bleak future. This realization left them adrift on a sea of loneliness, but now purpose anchored them, engaged them in something great. By delivering this devastating blow, glory would be theirs, at last.

For much of their life, they'd wandered the kingdom, directionless. Now, on this night, a warmth spread within.

I'm special, chosen by the goddess herself. What a privilege.

Years taught them that fresh wood from the hazel tree made a good weapon against mediocrity. Achiel raised the glass on the Five-Feather Crown. No alarm sounded. The guards' presence served to dispel thieves for years. Besides, no one would dare touch the goddess's items for fear of immediate death. Not Achiel, for they acted in the goddess's will.

With a flick of their wrists, Achiel conjured the wind's power once more.

Levitate.

The glass hovered, spinning above the pedestal. With a

quick rush, Achiel swept the crown into the sack and attached it to their back. Finally, their magic warranted divine purpose, not scorn from The Order.

"Hoot! Stop!" the female guard shouted.

Achiel spun around to face them. *So, they're not ignorant sheep!*

The guards ran forward, but with a sweep of their hand, Achiel sent a tight wind bolt into the woman. Like a giant fist, the gust knocked her back into the wall. Her outstretched arms knocked over the items on the table positioned just inside the door. A water pitcher, parchments, and a bowl crashed to the floor.

The male raised his wooden baton high into the air. "Stop! Put down the sack!"

Achiel yawned. They put down the sack as directed. "I'm leaving here, with the crown."

The male guard shook his head. "By the goddess, you dare!"

Achiel laughed and pushed their palms outward toward the guard. "And I'm still alive!"

"Step away," the guard commanded. He stepped forward with his baton raised. "Don't move."

Achiel closed their eyes and visualized the power churning in their core. As they did so, their hands moved in circular motions, gathering the magic into small wind whirls. Their hands moved faster, becoming a blur.

Achiel opened their eyes and cackled. "I will touch whatever I want, but you won't."

Less than ten feet separated them now, and Achiel released the two whirling winds.

"*Coupe!*"

Those rapid spinning winds acted like saws and sliced through the guard's wrists, his baton clambering to the floor. Blood splattered across the neighboring exhibits. The guard screamed and collapsed to the ground.

Achiel scooped up the sack, suppressed a laugh, and disappeared into the night.

CHAPTER ONE

TWO DAYS LATER

The University of Sulidae was the oldest college in Aves. Originally, its location resided in the Audubon Nest, close to Lanham, home of The Order. Political infighting forced the intellectuals to put some distance between themselves and those at court. Experience taught them that the closer one got to power, the harder it was to survive. In response, The Order opened an intelligence file on university members. Despite the history of hurt feelings and tensions on both sides, many of those within The Order's rank traveled and studied at the university's new location in Sulidae Egg, in Edmonds Nest. It sat on the banks of the Plume River at the apex of the Audubon and Edmonds nests. The campus was its own island in the egg; everything revolved around the university.

Rook Bjorn Renner's entire life orbited around Sulidae University, most importantly the Museum of the Goddess. As curator, Rook Renner's true passion to which his entire life was devoted was collecting goddess artifacts. As a renowned expert in all things goddess, he received a consistent stream of requests to verify and validate recently discovered treasures. Over time, his teachings gained more urgency around authenticity.

Prentice found it strange that a devoted bird like Rook Renner would steal the Five-Feathered Crown. Why now? Why only that artifact? Why not something less obvious? He wouldn't be able to get birdsong for the relic. No one would take the risk of being caught with it. No one would dare touch the crown for fear of death.

The theft didn't add up.

Hawk Prentice Tasifa sat on the train speeding from Gould to Sulidae. She picked up Cardinal Wick's letter and read it again.

Hawk Tasifa—

Your services have been requested in the Sulidae Egg. Arrive within two days and greet Dove Raz Haq. The situation as we know at this time:

Missing sacred goddess's feathered crown.

Proposed magical use.

Possible suspects: Rook Bjorn Renner.

The truth is light. Bring it forth as hawks see what is unseen.

Peace,

Cardinal Wick

She rolled the parchment up again.

Someone *did* break into the museum, and they stole the

Five-Feathered Crown. In the ensuing massive manhunt, the eagles who served as security for all eggs searched but came up empty. Request for assistance from the public produced nothing, according to the reports. No doubt, Rook Renner was frantic with worry and he stood accused of stealing it himself.

Prentice sipped her tea as ideas formulated in her mind. Drinking Earl Grey became a simple pleasure among the stickiness of investigative work. The ancient cogwheel train raced across the rails, and it gently rocked as it chugged its way through the Edmonds Nest. She'd left the Bailey's rolling hills and the Adams Mountains with their snow-capped tips. They had grown smaller in the distance along with Bailey Egg's red-roofed buildings.

Now, two days later, she meandered along the Adams River. She missed Gould, and if the circumstances changed, she'd return again, but not for work.

Prentice had the sleeping car to herself, an ornately decorated car whose features included carved wood paneling, pressed metal ceiling, frosted glass, lamp oils, and a night seat that folded down for a bed. Over the last couple of days, the car had started to feel like home. She sat in the small, overstuffed chair and removed her notepad.

When not on an active investigation, Prentice wore casual clothing; her dark wings identified her as a hawk no matter what she wore. Today she had chosen a sapphire headdress that bore silver embroidered wings and matched her frock. A silver satin scarf draped from her neck across her left shoulder. She put away the boots in exchange for flat, closed-toe sandals. Sulidae lay in the Edmonds Nest, just southwest of Lanham. The weather remained warm throughout the year due to the Avian Sea currents. She dressed accordingly, but only by chance. Unable to return home from her last assignment for a change of clothes, Prentice happened to have packed cooler clothing.

Ahead, Sulidae Egg appeared. Her thoughts turned to Rook Renner. No doubt, the rook sowed the seeds of his own demise with his erratic behavior.

The train bumped over the railroad tracks as it slowed into Lizard Mountain Train Station, with the setting sun. A whistle announced their arrival, and Prentice disembarked with her luggage and satchel. Along the platform, coachmen carried signs advertising their services. She secured one and found herself quickly seated in a carriage, her luggage bags secured outside in the rear, her driver holding the reins in front. Two beautiful horses pulled them away from the train station and into the waiting night.

In what seemed like no time, she reached campus. Being early suppertime, the egg bustled with life. Students clutched heavy satchels and walked or bicycled through the streets. People clustered together in casual conversations at outdoor cafes, illuminated by lanterns' warm glow. Pedestrians hiked alongside cyclists with ease in a practiced rhythm.

In the hushed carriage interior, Prentice embraced the nostalgia rushing over her. She hadn't been here in years, not since graduation. Outside the carriage window, the Plume River glistened as it snaked its way alongside the egg. A clear sky put the constellations on display, and she warmed at the memory of nights spent in Rook Ioan's astronomy class, charting, and memorizing the heavens, gazing through telescopes, and listening to how they came to be. A hawk was never lost as long as they had the sky.

"We're here." The coachman wrenched open the door and disappeared around to the carriage's rear. He clambered up the short ladder and threw down her luggage bags. They smacked the ground.

"By the goddess, be careful!" Prentice bellowed as she exited. *Vultures!*

The coachman came back around with said baggage stuffed under both arms. He glared at her as he placed the bags beside her. His tight, grayish skin bore thin scars. The bright scarlet birthmark across his sharp nose drew attention away from his dark beady eyes.

"Thank you." Prentice took five birdsongs from her leather pouch. She dropped the copper coin with the five emblazon on the tail and the goddess's likeness on the front into the coachman's gloved hand.

"Evening." The man bowed, his face softened by the tip, before leaping up to the driver's seat. His agility surprised her; his girth didn't hinder his movements at all.

She turned her attention to the pristine cathedral that consumed the center entrance of the university campus. The air was heavy with the fragrance of frankincense and sage. A cobblestoned maze of dark corridors threaded through the grounds and connected the buildings. Dark hallways stretched out in a monolithic maze of nooks and crannies, making it impossible to take in the enormity of the university at a glance.

Ahead, a figure approached through the growing dark. Brightly colored lanterns illuminated the square and entranceway. She could make out a red turban atop a head. A sudden strong wind billowed dark robes. Prentice didn't need her hawk abilities to recognize Rook Renner. Her jaw tightened as he advanced.

Once the wizened old man reached her, he wasted no time embracing her.

"Hoot, Prentice." Renner pulled her close.

His voice was stronger than Prentice expected.

She returned his hug but pulled back. "Hoot, Rook! How are you here? Shouldn't you be in a cell?"

Rook Renner's jovial face held bemusement. He didn't seem distraught. "It would seem my rapidly eroding reputation has kept that action at bay."

His rawboned features, decorated with broad red lines beneath each eye and a vertical one from his forehead down to his chin, disappeared beneath a bushy white beard.

"Come. I'm glad you're here." He clasped her hand in his bony one. His soft palm spoke to the rook never doing physical labor in his life.

"Me too." She meant it.

He motioned ahead. "I've had a small instructor apartment set up for you."

Prentice took back her hand. "An apartment? Rook, you know I'm here to investigate you and the theft…"

She trailed off. A shiver filtered through her feathers.

Rook Renner raised his hand. The silver rings he wore caught the pale moonlight as he held his hand up to silence her.

"I'm aware. It's a studio, nothing luxurious. The Order cannot say I attempted to bribe you. My status may not be what it once was at court, but I'm greatly injured at this intrusion. The sooner we get this resolved, the sooner I can get back to my work."

"Rook…" Prentice's cheeks warmed at his words.

But she didn't travel here to rekindle their student-instructor relationship. She'd been assigned to this case, and she had a job to do.

See the unseen.

She adjusted her satchel across her torso and then hoisted her luggage.

"Lead the way."

Rook Renner smiled. "Follow me."

CHAPTER TWO

The ground-floor studio apartment held all the creature comforts Prentice expected from a faculty living space. Her new quarters were comprised of a single expansive room, including a space off the primary living section for a bathroom—complete with a compact tub, a tiny, square ceramic sink, and clean towels. Prentice dropped her luggage inside the doorway. She turned to Rook Renner.

"This is great. Thank you."

"You must be peckish. Come down to the student dining hall for supper. It's still time to grab something." Rook Renner squeezed her shoulder.

"Sure." Prentice took the key from him, locked the door, and followed him through the building's front entranceway and out to the cobblestone campus grounds.

The campus remained shrouded in the early evening twilight, turning the daytime hustle and bustle into a dreamy landscape. The sprawling complex conveyed a sense of mystery cloaked in hushed conversations, whispered giggles, and magic. The rook continued to walk with her.

"Prentice, I may not be around to say this, so I'm saying this now. I had nothing to do with the theft. Once Dove Haq becomes involved, our contact will be limited," Rook Renner said.

Prentice frowned at him. "Spit it out, Rook. Don't be cagey."

She would meet with the dove early the next morning. The dove managed all aspects of the egg's government. Still, she wondered if this was more of the rook's light-hearted sense of humor? The rook's demeanor changed. He didn't look so much like himself.

Rook Renner stroked his beard. "It has, no doubt, occurred to you that I may be killed to be silenced?"

Prentice stopped. "What do you know that would get you killed?"

He gave her a weary smile. "I've been around many years. You have to ask yourself, why was the crown stolen now?"

Prentice hated when rooks answered questions with another question. They started walking again toward the dining hall. Delicious aromas wafted toward them, rousing her hunger.

"Just tell me."

"Not here. The wind has ears. Go. Eat. Rest. We'll talk soon," Rook Renner said.

Prentice hesitated.

He had a non-violent personality, so his statement bothered her. She knew him well enough to know goading him wouldn't give her any results. Prentice had a feeling in her feathers, but she let it go. Something distracted him, and he displayed a marked fear.

Once they reached the dining hall, the rook disengaged and grew cold.

"This is where I leave you." Rook Renner bowed his head, turned on his sandaled feet, and left, leaving a confused Prentice in his wake.

She entered the dining area but found the seating space brimming with people. This made sense given the sparsely populated grounds; all the birds had flocked together in there. The tawny walls bore murals of the goddess's creation stories, former owls, and Sulidae's lush landscape with its rich culture of fishing and agriculture. Prentice got into the serving line behind others, memories of student life coming back to her. A row of brightly coiffed males, dressed in short-sleeved tunics and loose pants covered by aprons, scooped stew into wooden bowls. Gloved students passed the bowls across to those in the line. Prentice opted for roasted tomato and rice. It'd been flavored with oregano and bits of beef.

She took a section of warm potato bread, fresh baked and delicious, from a platter at the end of the serving line. Prentice followed the others to the paying lines at the front of the kitchen. Two older females, who looked exhausted, took birdsong. Prentice paid her one birdsong and remarked how inexpensive the food was. The university benefitted from donations and monetary support from The Order.

Threading her way through the tight maze of tables, conversations, and shifting motions, she found a spot toward the corner rear of the dining hall. The front of the seating area had a huge hearth for those colder desert nights. The intense aromas meshed in the heavy air creating an atmosphere of deliciousness that encouraged talking and relaxation. Alcohol had been forbidden on campus, but juice and water flowed freely. All kinds of birds from all parts of the kingdom joined together in clusters. Hawks, ostriches, young falcons, and cardinals shared meals and stories. The offspring from those elite sects engaged in animated conversations with those from outside The Order, joined together by shared love around certain studies and passions. A few young hawks tossed her favorable looks and spreading of wings in greeting.

Prentice took it all in, being sure to keep her back to a wall and her focus on the exits. She dug into her stew, tearing off thick chunks of bread to scoop the dark liquid. As she did so, her mind went back to those burning questions.

Who would steal the Five-Feathered Crown? Why? There hadn't been any requests for ransom, or any attempts to pawn it for funds. What did they plan to do with such an item? They could melt down its golden feathers, but that would require a blacksmith. She didn't know one who would risk the wrath of The Order to do it.

This case would force her to slog and slug her way through it. She trusted the fluttering in her feathers.

The chair across from Prentice scooted back, and a person lowered themselves into the vacant seat. She reached for her talons, and she cursed. They remained in her satchel, nestled on her lap, with the flap closed. She wouldn't be able to access them as fast as she wanted. She looked around and noted if she did bring them out, she could start a stampede in the dining hall.

Across from her, the man leaned on the table with his

elbows. He carried himself as if he would be up for anything, sizing her up, his red eyes crawling all over her. Sharp features and a reddish neck spoke to his nightjar lineage. He had full lips and a short nose and legs. His ivory turban matched the linen sheath he wore; a brown leather belt cinched the tunic around a narrow waist. He smelled of sandalwood and olive oil as he placed a bowl of salad greens and naan on the table.

"Hoot," he said.

"Hoot," Prentice replied. "Go. Away."

"You're a hawk," he said as if he hadn't heard her.

Prentice ate her stew but kept her gaze on her uninvited dinner guest. She didn't like crossing paths with people who knew more about her than she did them. His ruby red eyes gave her pause.

"You're the real deal. Right? Not in training like these others." He jerked his thumb to the crowded seating area.

Prentice ignored him.

"You've got that edge about you," he added.

Prentice put her spoon and bread in the stew bowl, adjusted her satchel, and stood up. *And yet, you sat down anyway.*

"Wait!" The guest stood up, too. "I'm Sebastian."

"So?" Prentice picked up her meal. She'd have a quiet environment back in her apartment.

"I work at the museum," he whispered and gestured her to sit down. "I want to talk."

"You do?"

"Yes, please sit down. I-I should've introduced myself first. I saw you with Rook Renner and followed you here."

"You followed me." Prentice lowered herself back into her seat.

"I didn't wanna interrupt your conversation. It looked serious."

She'd missed his shadowing, but she listened to Sebastian's rationale.

"What do you do at the museum? Are you a student?" She picked up her spoon and ate.

"No. I'm a guard, well, one of them. I wanted to meet you. I knew The Order assigned a hawk," Sebastian explained. He took his fork and sectioned off a chunk of his salad. The bowl brimmed with fresh-cut kale, cherry tomatoes, cucumber chunks, and sardines.

"Who told you this?" she said after swallowing another spoonful.

"Dove Raz Haq held a brief meeting in the library this morning. The museum is still sectioned off and closed. She told all of us."

"Who else is 'all of us'?" Prentice wondered how Rook Renner knew when she'd arrive. Few had access to her itinerary, but if the rook stood accused of stealing the crown, why did he continue to be free and privy to the investigation?

Sebastian swallowed. "The remaining staff. The evening guards are still in medical."

Prentice recalled the violent details of the theft from the report. Two guards, armed only with wooden batons, patrolled the three-thousand-square-foot space. The morning after the theft's discovery, both guards had suffered severe injuries. One of the guards struck her head on the pavement, hit from behind. The thief bashed her head in.

The second guard got into a scuffle that erupted into a violent brawl. He suffered. His hands had been severed at the wrists. If there was one thing experience taught her, it was that a cornered burglar was a dangerous thing. A lesson someone should've told the guard. Even now, two days later, he still fought for his life with aid from the healers, hovering near death from the blood loss. Why would a thief spend time beating and fighting? Theft involved stealth and fast execution with no witnesses to avoid confrontation. The perpetrator laid in ambush. Robberies didn't look like this. Despite the burglary having already occurred, something more brewed beneath the seemingly straightforward surface. She had a feeling of foreboding and knew there had to be more.

"Where you there? That evening?" Prentice asked.

Sebastian looked around before answering. "No. I worked the morning shift. I, I found them when I got there. It was the most gruesome thing I'd ever seen."

When he glanced up at her, his eyes were glazed over.

"I see," Prentice said.

He didn't look at her as he pushed lettuce around his bowl. "Do you? When the sun goes down, this can be a scary place. I know hawks are supposed to see the unseen, but could anyone have spied this coming?"

"I'm a graduate of the university, as are all hawks. I lived on the campus as I'm sure you're aware." She quirked an eyebrow at him. Like other large eggs, Sulidae had pockets of crime. That danger rarely encroached on the university's grounds and judging by the dining room's atmosphere, the students hadn't been impacted by the museum incident.

Sebastian snapped his head up at her subtle rebuke.

"I'm sorry, hawk. I meant no offense. It's just..."

"What?" Prentice prodded.

"...I was supposed to work that night, but I switched shifts with Helena. When I found them, time stood still."

Prentice's wooden spoon scraped the bowl's bottom. Disappointed, she drank some water to wash down the rest of the meal. *The food wasn't this good when I studied here.* She contemplated going for another bowl. The train food left much to be desired.

"Hawk?" Sebastian said. "You look like you wanted to say something."

"Yes. Tell me what you saw when you arrived at work."

Sebastian hesitated. "I gave a statement to the eagles already."

"Then tell me," Prentice said. She'd follow up with the Sulidae eagles tomorrow.

"It was all pretty shocking. I came into the museum. The front desk was in disarray. Parchments from Rook Renner's office were scattered across the exhibit floor. Shards of glass from the water pitcher scattered all over the place. I-I found Helena and Pranske. I screamed at the top of my lungs for help. Someone heard my frantic hollering. I can't remember who. The others streamed in, and someone, I dunno who, called the eagles. Campus healers arrived. It's kind of a blur."

"There wasn't anything else taken?"

Sebastian shook his head, eyes averted. "The rook said no. I didn't see anything else missing. I tried not to look, to be honest with you."

Sebastian's gruesome discovery added a labyrinth of more questions to an already long list. This thief acted elusive and impulsive. The eagles stated they scoured the area for evidence. She'd dig into what they found and would discover what they missed.

"It was weird." Sebastian's voice wavered as he spoke just above the din.

"What was weird?" Prentice sat up straight in her seat.

He shrugged. "When I first got there, the air tasted funny, strange. You know the museum maintains a certain mixture to preserve the artifacts and a filtration system to keep things from drying out or from being too moist."

Prentice nodded. The museum used a complex system of linen and fans to keep the exhibits at the correct temperature. A thermostat monitored it.

"I've been working there for years, so I'm used to the change in the air, but that morning, it was just *different*."

Prentice made a note of it and got up from the table. "Good evening, Sebastian."

He didn't look up. He remained hunched over his full salad bowl.

CHAPTER THREE

The next morning, Prentice bounded up the stairs to Dove Raz Haq's anteroom. She entered a cool and quiet atmosphere, unlike the woman herself. She had an energy about her that drew people. Raz Haq oversaw the church members of her egg, Sulidae. That encompassed those at the university including students, faculty, and staff. While some doves' eggs barely scratched three thousand people, Sulidae approached fifteen thousand, five times that number. They were required to follow the rules. Including those of the outer shell, birds that resided outside Sulidae Egg. They didn't follow the goddess's teachings, but on campus, they were required to follow the rules.

Dove Raz Haq rounded the corner, and out of the blue, the atmosphere changed. Dark, smooth, flawless skin made luminous by light peered out from beneath an ivory headdress embroidered around its edges with dark red shapes representing the various Aves bird sects. She swept into the attached anteroom with her flowing tunic and matching shalwar kameez. The tunic's bell sleeves bore the same shapes as her headdress. Dove Haq had beautiful white teeth and a dimpled smile. Blue-silver curly hair, like cotton, billowed from beneath her headdress.

When she spoke, her ceremonious tone echoed down to Prentice's soul. All doves had a vocal power to help them calm and soothe their flocks and the occasional ruffled feathers. But Dove Raz Haq had crafted hers into a true talent.

In a word, she was stunning.

Prentice recalled why she harbored a crush on the dove throughout her years at the university.

"Hoot, Prentice Tasifa. It's been a while," Dove Haq said in way of greeting. "I remember when you attended our university."

"Yes, Dove. Hoot." The dove's voice forced a shiver down Prentice's wings. She suppressed the urge to shudder.

"This has put a big fear on campus. I'm surprised they sent such a young hawk to investigate such a complex mystery as this." Dove Haq adjusted her sleeves, revealing leather bracelets along her wrists.

"I'm a fifth-year investigator. As I understand it, Rook Renner stands accused of the theft," Prentice said. The dove's comments only served to steel her resolve in finding the culprit.

The dove standing before her scoffed. "Initially, yes, but disturbing evidence arrived a day before you did. His life hung by a thread, but thankfully, we were able to prevent damage to the individual, Rook Renner."

"What disturbing evidence?" Prentice realized things could change in the two travel days it took for her to arrive in Sulidae. What stuck in her craw? That no one from The Order bothered to tell her. She always had her bird caller on her person.

Dove Haq shook her head. "Rook Renner wouldn't be capable of shearing off someone's hands."

"No? He looks healthy to me," Prentice said.

The dove rolled her gorgeous eyes. "Tsk, and they say hawks can see the unseen..."

"In all fairness, Dove, I haven't been to the scene, and I'm three days behind."

"What's this? Excuses?"

Prentice stiffened at the rebuke.

"The exonerating factor for Rook Renner was the thief used wind magic," Dove Haq continued. "Which, I'm sure even you know, is forbidden."

"Wind magic hasn't been documented in Aves for what, a hundred years?" Prentice took out her notepad from one of the pouches on her utility belt along with a small pencil she used to scratch out notes.

Dove Haq met Prentice's incredulousness with a warning.

"I'll introduce you to the staff, but proceed with caution, Prentice. Speak not of the wind magic—that hasn't been disclosed to anyone, not even Rook Renner. Only those in the higher echelons of The Order, myself, and now, you, know."

"And the thief," Prentice added.

Dove Haq gave her a small smile. "Oh, yes, and the thief."

Prentice followed the dove from her internal anteroom and down a short corridor toward her office. Dove Haq had an assistant and a university director. Prentice didn't see either of those individuals present. As if hearing her thoughts, Dove Haq spoke over her shoulder.

"I must reiterate the need to keep this contained. The last thing the university needs is a scandal. Discretion is a necessity. Report to me. No one else. To starve the rumor mill, I'm handling this directly."

"Understood." Prentice nodded.

"Great. Follow me." Dove Haq gestured to the wooden door.

She gracefully swept into a copious room. Her presence silenced the agitated murmurs of a few moments before. To Prentice's right stood a round, brushed oak desk complete with inkwell, quill, and parchment. A wicker basket crammed with scrolls sat at the feet of a cushioned high-back chair. Adjacent to the desk stood floor-to-ceiling high bookshelves, which continued around the room. Prentice counted fifteen in all. Windows had been placed along opposite walls, and the shorter shelves contained potted plants. Natural light poured in from the windows and the skylight.

At the room's center, beneath the skylight, an Edmonds-style rug stretched out in a sea of dark crimson, embellished with golden curlicues, paisleys, and circles. Large, square pillows of royal blues and golds dotted the floor.

"Everyone, this is Hawk Tasifa. She's here to investigate the crown's disappearance. I'm sure you'll give her your complete cooperation."

"Thank you, Dove. Hoot, everyone. I'm Prentice," Prentice said with a wave. She walked over to the three staff members seated on the rug. She lowered herself onto one of the available pillows.

"Hoot," Sebastian said. He sat to Prentice's left. He peered at her through half-closed eyes. As a nightjar, he struggled with mornings.

The ostrich seated directly in front of Prentice bore a bemused expression. She sat with her thick legs extended in front of her and crossed at the ankles. Her long, soft, blue frock sported a high collar, which revealed her blue neck. She had a bald head decorated with spiked metal piercings that shot out the sides of her head like axles on a wheel, curving around the ear instead of protruding. Large luminous eyes studied Prentice.

"I'm Killion Oyange," she said. "I'm the museum's conservator."

Prentice nodded in greeting. To her right sat another female, but this one towered over all of them. Only Killion came close, and she remained several inches shorter. The woman bore gray skin adorned with darkly lined eyes and deep, purple-stained lips. A long, satiny headdress fell to just below her shoulders and a silk tunic with an embroidered V-neck matched her pants. Despite the scent of an expensive perfume, she had a body odor, one of death. *Carrion.*

A vulture. Here? Prentice kept her face blank.

"I'm Zell Magero. I'm the archivist." The timbre in her voice made Prentice's feathers rustle.

She didn't smile. "Uneasy, hawk? Vultures can do more than act as funeral directors and servants. Although we come from humble beginnings, we can still soar."

Prentice forced a smile. "Of course. Now, I'd like to ask you some questions."

Zell sat upright. "We've already given our statements to the eagles."

"Yes, and now, I'll ask you additional questions," Prentice said, with a nod. "I understand this may cause some grim talk, but be clear, concise, and thorough in your answers. I don't have to tell you how important this is for the kingdom."

"If it's so important, why did it take you two days to get here? Lanham is only a few hours away by train," Zell asked.

"I just concluded an appointment in Gould," Prentice replied.

Killion's eyes widened. "Gould? That's all the way north, in Adams's Nest."

"Yes, it is," Prentice said, surprised that she knew the tiny egg's location.

"Why didn't they send someone from Lanham?" Zell asked, drawing Prentice's attention back to her.

Prentice didn't know, and she'd wondered the same thing herself.

"It doesn't matter. She's here, now," Sebastian said, piping up from the other side of Prentice.

Killion rubbed her arms. "The whole thing disturbed me."

Sebastian chimed in. "The blood. It's stuck in my mind."

Zell said, "If you don't catch him, you know he'll do it again."

An alarm bell went off in Prentice's head. "Why do you think it's a male?"

Zell hitched up her chin. She struggled for an answer before blurting out, "Only a male would put on such a flamboyant display of violence and savagery. This was a perverse crime, born of attention-seeking hijinks."

"Nothing about this was natural," Killion interjected softly. She had her gaze pinned on Prentice. "Right, hawk?"

One thing Prentice knew at once: Killion knew how to flirt. She had a way of drawing people in, and Sebastian chief among them. Each time she spoke, he piped up from his slumped posture to lean in and listen.

Prentice raised her hands, palms out. "Let me ask the questions. Okay?"

Zell crossed her arms and huffed.

"First question, where were you on Tuesday, Canari 7th?"

Prentice turned the page on her notepad.

Sebastian started first. "I was at the museum. I arrived at work at 7 a.m. I encountered a horrifying sight and I checked Helena and Pranske. I shouted for the rook to call the eagles."

Prentice got a cold feeling. "Rook Renner was there?"

"He arrived a breath after I did. He was just outside his office door," Sebastian said.

"What about you?" Prentice looked over at Zell and Killion.

"When I arrived at nine, the entire museum had been roped off. I couldn't get inside, so I didn't see anything," Killion explained. "I did see them bring out poor Pranske and Helena, but that's all. A crowd of students and instructors gathered around the entranceway, so I couldn't see much more."

"What did you do afterward?" Prentice asked.

"Well, um, I went to see Dove Haq, who had gathered the four of us in a room at the library. It was there she told us about what happened. I-I didn't know about the sheer brutality of the attack until then."

"All right, and you, Zell?" Prentice asked.

"*Professor* Magero," she rebutted.

"Professor Magero, please, tell me where you were when the attack on the museum happened?" Prentice gripped her pencil so hard it snapped. She fished through her pouch to retrieve another one.

"I was on my way to work, when the crown was stolen, and the guards attacked. When I arrived, Rook Renner was on the floor beside Pranske, and he had what looked like the bathroom towels compressed against Pranske's hands, um arms. Once the eagles arrived, we were all swept into Rook Renner's office and detained there with an armed eagle. After what felt like forever, Dove Haq came and took me and Sebastian to the library room where we met up with Killion."

"The whole thing is just so unsettling," Killion whispered, clutching the front of her frock.

"We're all floored by the crown's theft. Who would dare?" Zell said, her eyes narrowed, her hands balled into fists.

Prentice met Killion's eyes and noted that beneath the budding instructor's sweet demeanor, an edge poked through, like a blade hidden in feathers. It raised her suspicions. As for Zell, Prentice knew through experience that vultures rubbed shoulders with some dangerous, shady, dirty birds. She didn't expect vultures to be practicing wind users, but the whole incident spoke to professionals. It had been planned and premeditated.

"All right, next question. Did any of you see anything out of the ordinary? It doesn't matter how small the detail. Anything at all? Please, think before you answer. Close your eyes and revisit that day," Prentice said gently.

After several long minutes, Zell said, "It was so senseless."

"I thought I was going to faint," Sebastian whispered, breathing heavily.

Prentice suppressed a sigh. *These trees aren't bearing fruit.*

"Thank you all for your help." Prentice stood up and closed her notepad. She returned it and the pencil to her pouch.

Startled, the three staff members looked at each other and then to Prentice.

"That's it?" Killion asked, plucked eyebrows rose high.

"Yes. I'll be in touch with each of you, later. Are you all staying on campus?" Prentice asked.

Sebastian shook his head. "I don't live on campus, but the rook and dove have my information."

Killion said, "I live in faculty housing with my partner."

Zell nodded. "I also live in faculty housing."

"Good. I know where to find you." Prentice made a beeline toward the dove's office door with a sense of urgency pressing against her back. These three didn't witness anything of value, or so they said. Yet she couldn't shake the feeling they hadn't told her everything. Her best source of information would be the scene itself and the two guards who engaged with the thief.

CHAPTER FOUR

Prentice exited the dove's office via a side door that led to an alleyway between the dove's patronage and the church and into broad daylight. The early morning fog had long since burned off. The 11 a.m. bell toned, reminding students not already in class of their tardiness. It had a distinctive sound. Several such individuals scampered by her as they made mad dashes through open doors and past her in the alley. Two female students barreled out of an ornate black carriage, nearly colliding as they raced to their studies. Prentice chuckled, but soon sobered.

Three days gone. Was the thief poised to strike again? Demand a ransom?

She headed to the medical center. The entire case slipped between her fingers like sand. Already late to the scene, Prentice realized she needed to create a chronology of the suspects.

First, she had to speak to the witnesses. They were valuable clues the thief had left alive. Helena and Pranske survived the ordeal, but they incurred injuries and emotional and physical scars. Prentice steeled herself for the work ahead. There are details you shouldn't know, and once you do, it's hard to silence them. Cutting off a person's hands implied they had stolen something. What had Pranske done to warrant such a violent response from the thief?

Despite what Dove Haq said, fear hovered over the shaken university. Prentice's razor-sharp instincts heard the noise. The questions escaped in whispers and nervous laughter.

Would the thief strike again?

Prentice needed evidence, a clue, something to push the investigation toward conclusion.

So, she'd delve deeper.

As she approached the medical building, a horrible feeling took over.

The bleak backdrop of The Geese of Golden Ridge felt at odds with the bright yellow smocks the raven doctors and geese assistants wore. Renowned for their intellect and knowledge, most healers came from ravens. They didn't follow the goddess's teachings. Instead, ravens focused on science and knowledge. Logic and research dictated their actions, so their bedside manners left much to be desired. That was where the geese came in. They assisted the ravens in healing and provided the comfort the doctors tended to lack.

"Hoot! I'm Hawk Prentice Tasifa," Prentice introduced herself once she reached the geese information desk. "I'm here to see Helena and Pranske."

"Yes. We were expecting you. Dove Haq called ahead," Doctor Usue said. Her locked hair had been pulled back into a loose bun. She had gorgeous dark skin, smooth with hints of warmth on her high cheekbones. "Follow me."

Doctor Usue started down the hall, making a right, and then a left.

"How bad are they?" Prentice asked as they walked.

"Helena suffered blunt force trauma to the head," the healer confirmed.

"Is she awake?"

"Yes."

"And Pranske?"

"He's two doors down and still in a coma." She paused, turning to look at Prentice. "Magic injuries are horribly difficult to heal. That's why he's in an induced coma. We are having to transfer blood to him every twelve hours. His condition is critical."

That pointed to a cruel reality. The bird who stole the crown also wielded magic, wind magic, according to the dove. The doctor's comments about Pranske's injuries spoke to the same.

"Will he recover?" Prentice wanted to talk to him.

Dr. Usue pressed her lips into a fine line. "I can't predict his fate. He's alive, but critical, as I said."

"I understand."

Doctor Usue's expression said she didn't believe it, but she didn't speak it aloud. They continued to Helena's room. They approached the hushed, cracked doorway. Doctor Usue ushered Prentice in.

"Be gentle. Go slow. If she gets too upset, you're done." With that, she headed back down the hallway.

Everyone was quiet because everyone was in pain.

Prentice entered the narrow room. It smelled like other healing places; doused in a mixture of copper, tart herbs, and smoldering sage. The hint of death clung to the odor's underbelly like sap on a sandal.

Helena lay in her single-size bed, covered with blankets. Bandages covered her forehead, her forearms, and her hands. She had defensive wounds, so she had fought. Prentice recalled Sebastian's statement about finding both guards bloodied and battered.

"Hoot, Helena," Prentice called softly as to not spook the woman. Prentice crept farther into the room. She halted at the end of the bed and removed her notepad and pencil. "Hoot, Helena."

Someone had braided Helena's hair that stuck out from beneath the bandage. She wore a medical smock with short sleeves. The thin cotton blankets covered her from mid-torso to the end of the bed. Her arms rested on top.

"Hoot," Helena croaked. A big green eye watched Prentice with interested trepidations. She tried to sit up.

"Calm yourself. Be calm. I'm Hawk Tasifa." Prentice introduced herself. "I have a few questions about the incident. Is that okay?"

"Yes." Helena pushed herself to an upright position. She clenched her hands in pain. "You talk like it wasn't an unimaginable horror."

"That's why I'm here. To learn, so take your time."

"It's hard to judge the time." She stretched out her hand, hissing as she did so.

"Pranny and me were doing our sweep. We do it every half an hour. When we returned to the entranceway, we discovered the thief."

"Did you rattle the thief? You didn't hear or see anything strange before that?"

"No. Nothing. We swept the museum at closing, including the restrooms."

She swallowed and took her glass of water from a tiny square table. She guzzled it down greedily. It spilled over the corners of her mouth and down her chin. Without wiping her mouth, she continued.

"We ordered them to stop. Pleaded..."

"Them? There were two of them?" Prentice interjected. She peered up from her notepad.

"I dunno gender. I couldn't tell." Helena's voice began to shake. Tears welled in her eyes. "It happened so fast. They were covered from head to toe in beige clothing. They didn't speak, only attacked, a vicious and jarring attack..." She shuddered. "A searing heat erupted in my head."

"You're doing good," Prentice coaxed. "Can you tell me anything that could help me catch this person?"

"Whomever they were, they were driven by a violent passion and the magic used was like a breeze, like wind. The thief floated up in the air, and what they did to, to..."

Prentice went around to comfort Helena.

"Hush. Be calm. You're safe."

Helena dissolved into hysterics, and she couldn't be consoled. The guard relived the horrifying and grisly event; one of the most revolting things she'd ever seen. Prentice watched as Helena tumbled down into the memory. The wound remained too new. At the noise and shouts, two yellow-clad geese hurried in. They forced Prentice out of the room and into the hallway. One of them slammed the door shut.

Prentice walked down a few doors until she discovered Pranske. True to the doctor's words, he remained in a coma. Around his bed, ivory candles formed a protective barrier. Various herbs from the apothecary draped from the ceiling above his body. Soft chanting emitted from a speaker beside his bed. Now wrapped in such a peaceful environment, Pranske had suffered such violence. Why? Was it an attempt at scaremongering? If so, to whom was the vile message directed? Did the assailant have a connection to Pranske? If so, what? The assailant wanted people to see what they'd done, what they're capable of doing.

Instead of disturbing him, Prentice turned her attention to the museum.

Still too many questions and not enough answers.

She needed concrete evidence. Conjecture wouldn't placate Dove Haq or The Order. The case had too many moving parts. The entire affair made her sick. As she made her way across campus, she passed the dining hall. The aroma of delicious food wafted out and snared her attention. She followed her belly's suggestion and entered.

After going through the line and selecting her lunch choice, Prentice found the seating area less full than last night's dinner crowd. She spied Killion seated in a four-person booth along the bank of windows.

"Hoot, Killion," Prentice said.

Killion looked up from her hummus salad. "Oh, hoot, hawk."

The instructor's warm greeting faded at record speed. She dropped her gaze back to the parchment in front of her.

"May I join you?" Prentice asked.

"Yes." Killion didn't look up. Her finger traced the words sprawled in elegant script across the parchment.

Prentice placed her own bowl on the table and slid into

the booth. She poured a glass of water from the table's shared pitcher. While the silence continued, Prentice ate her lunch. Should she dismantle the wall or let it be?

She wouldn't get answers if she didn't ask questions.

"What are you reading?" Prentice asked.

"My lecture notes. I have class in a few minutes," she replied. Killion looked up at last.

"About?"

"Today's lecture will discuss the forward-thinking beliefs of the goddess," Killion explained, placing both manicured claws on the table.

"Ah, so the pillars?" Prentice drank her water.

"Deeper than the surface discourse around the three pillars." Killion scoffed. "The goddess in all her wisdom spoke about the centering of women and our power. Harnessing women's inner strength, our natural leadership skills, and the five we conjure," Killion explained. "Men are helpless without the guiding arm of women."

Prentice had heard these interpretations of the goddess's teachings before. The Order didn't support them, but it did allow and encourage academic discourse.

"Those are strong words," Prentice said. "They reek of generalizations and male bias."

Killion, now embolden, shrugged. "Students enjoy debates. It encourages logic and weeds out fallacies and emotional opinion that enflame and confuse people to believe they're facts."

"Yes, but do *you* believe it?"

"Think on it," Killion replied. "With males, evil emerges again and again as history explains. Who maintains The Order in Aves? The females do, from the low-ranking condors to the high flying and wise owls."

"Yet, the goddess maintains a regimen of hard work, eliminates evil desires." Prentice stabbed the last bit of salad.

"Males have nothing to shore up their weakness of violence," Killion continued. "Take Sebastian, for example. He bicycles to work and lives near Beacon State Park. He's withdrawn from his family due to early childhood trauma. Thus, he's alienated from his father because of it. He dresses like a beggar. All of his issues and poverty are results of his father's treatment on the family. With his lack of funds, he could possibly steal the crown."

"You suspect him?"

"Don't you? I mean, he's a nightjar. They're only good for thieving and assassinations."

"Why hire him and Pranske to guard the museum? They're both nightjars."

Killion shrugged. "Who better than those familiar with the trade?"

"How do you know so much about him?" Prentice sat back in the seat.

Killion patted her mouth with a cloth napkin. "I was on the hiring committee. He's a nightjar. Perfect for evening shifts."

"So why would he volunteer to switch to an early morning shift?"

Killion stood and collected her notes. "I don't know, but ask him. Maybe Pranske plied him with drinks."

As the spotlight shifted from her, Killion became less warm. She required someone to fawn over her.

"Gotta go!" Killion tossed over her shoulder as she strolled away.

Prentice left the dining hall a short while later and made her way across campus to the Museum of the Goddess. The crime was a targeted hit. The thief burst onto the scene and sunk back into the shadows. But how?

The entrance doors had been roped off as well as the perimeter around the museum. The neighboring library, attached via a shared hallway, had lost an entrance point, and several students approached the doors, spied its closure, and retreated in complaints. Prentice watched them come and go, but she didn't really see them.

She had work to do here.

"Who are you?" She didn't expect an answer.

When the traffic around the museum died down, Prentice summoned her hawk abilities by closing her eyes and invoking the mental incantation. A word in for it in the high speech didn't exist. The blood magic to see the unseen had been bred so thoroughly into her people, they no longer had a word for it.

When she opened her eyes, the building blurred, smearing until the joining of her human vision and hawk stabilized, and she could see all the perspectives—ahead, beside, and below.

She spied mysterious droplets along the exit door from the museum. They formed a disturbing pattern in the now-cleaned blood on the flat stone stairs. She dipped under the roped-off section and into the building and stood at the museum's entrance. Streak marks stirred in the minute dust. Whose blood was it? Pranske? Barefoot prints on the floor's residual dust. They'd removed their shoes. Bicycle tread marked the moist earth along the path.

She walked along the perimeter of the exhibit where the crown was stolen and bloodshed occurred. Finding the place impossibly clean, Prentice could only spy the faint hint of residue. With her arms folded, she watched the energy rise from the floor and the re-enactment of the heist unfold.

The thief had descended from the rafters. They had gone directly to the Five-Feathered Crown, and using wind magic, lifted its secured glass and removed it. The guards attacked. The spirits' muted shouting seemed as if they were miming the production, but Prentice had seen enough of these to know better. The thief used wind magic to shove Helena back against the wall, knocking her to the floor. Pranske raced forward to stop the thief, but wind magic was used to shear off his hands.

The thief, levitating, flew out of the museum, leaving the injured guards bleeding on the floor.

How did Helena get her defensive injuries? She didn't touch the thief.

Prentice noted that the injuries could've come from being tossed against the wall and smashing into the water pitcher and parchments. She made a mental note to follow up on it. Prentice didn't spy any additional notes about the theft. It would seem Helena and Sebastian had told her the truth.

Prentice exited the museum, slipped back under the ropes and out into the midday heat. She again noted the bicycle tracks in the sand, but many students biked. Carriage cost.

As soon as she ended her hawk sight, her human

eyesight faded. So she walked toward her apartment with her hawk vision on. Every detail, pore and feather, beak and claw, met with her scrutiny as she passed people. Her eyes couldn't help it. Instinct took over, and by the time she reached her building, she had to shut her abilities down from fatigue.

She found a bench outside the faculty apartments, waiting for her human vision to return. She heard the steps beside her, and she swung her talons out.

"Whoa! Whoa! Hawk Tasifa. It's me," Rook Renner said. "Calm yourself."

"Rook." Prentice re-holstered her guns. "What are you doing here?"

Prentice sat back and removed her hand-rolled cigarettes from a pouch on her utility belt. She snapped her fingers, and a small flame erupted from her index finger. She lit her cigarette and took a long drag. Shadows moved in front of her. Blurred bits of people. Although she couldn't see, she'd practiced the trick enough to do it, well, with her eyes closed.

"Mind if I join in?" Rook Renner asked.

"Not at all." Prentice exhaled a long stream of smoke. The muscles in her neck and shoulders relaxed. "You didn't come by the dove's office for questioning this morning."

"No, I had a lecture at that time," Rook Renner said.

She heard the unwrapping of a linen cloth. The rook's penchant for sweets hadn't changed. People thanked him with candy, which he kept in a linen cloth.

"Have you been to the medical building?" he asked.

"Yes," she said. "Awful business."

"Indeed. Any news of the crown?"

"Early days," she said. She kept the major obstacles to herself. "What do you know about wind magic?"

Rook Renner stroked his beard. "Wind magic, as you know, is a forbidden practice in Aves. When the goddess united the many birds into an order, she selected the owls for their wisdom and vision, the cardinals for their song and beauty, and the doves for their voice and calming qualities. Hawks, as you know, were elevated for their sight, fueled by their blood magic, and condors for their tenacity and strength."

Prentice nodded. "The five feathers comprise The Order."

"Yes. The other birds were relegated to the ground. Those practices of wind magic, that some birds used to fly, were outlawed."

"These birds included ostriches."

Rook Renner said, "Many of the wind practitioners reside here in the Edmonds Nest. Over the millennia, those numbers dwindled."

"But not gone."

Rook Renner fingered his beard. "Indeed."

"What about the staff? Let's start there."

"Yes, of course. I always liked Helena. She's humble and giving," Rook Renner said.

"And Pranske?"

"Pranny is a good guard," Rook Renner answered. "At first, I could sense a dark presence in him."

"You didn't dismiss him from his position?" Prentice said, smoking.

"He became frustrated when the joy he's been waiting for failed. He needed something to express his rage. So, I introduced him to one of the art students."

Prentice waited, enjoying her tobacco and the rook's deep, soothing voice.

"And Sebastian. He's a sensitive soul. He tries hard."

"You suspect none of them?" Prentice asked.

Rook Renner coughed out a hard laugh.

"I suspect all of them."

CHAPTER FIVE

Dove Haq crossed her legs and balanced her teacup and saucer inches above her knee. "I'm waiting for news of what you've learned."

"I found clues, but it's early days," Prentice answered.

"I know you hawks like to play it close to your breast, but I need answers. This news has residents reeling."

"I've got a feeling in my feathers about…"

"It's not professional to get carried away with a hunch, Hawk Tasifa."

The dove offered constant support to the flock. They looked to the charismatic dove for comfort. But not everyone was enthralled with her.

"Did you visit the guards?"

"One's in a coma. Yes?" Dove Haq sipped.

"Yes, but Helena is not only awake, but could use some comfort," Prentice replied.

Dove Haq nodded. "After morning service, I will visit them."

Prentice found it hard to fathom the dove's

heartlessness that she'd wait three days to visit those injured on her campus.

"If it makes you feel better, both my secretary and my assistant have visited and expressed my condolences."

Prentice could understand why.

"I have questions about Rook Renner."

Dove Haq gestured as if to say go on.

"Why was he considered a suspect?" Prentice asked.

The dove placed her teacup on its saucer. "You haven't spoken to the eagles."

"They're next on my list."

"I see." Dove Haq rubbed her hands over her silk, ivory pants. "What I'm about to tell you is confidential."

"Understood."

"It had come to my attention that Rook Renner may have been using museum funds to feather his own nest..."

"No!" Prentice waved it aside.

"...In recent months, several of his verified artifacts had been discovered, later, to be fakes. It appears Rook Renner started accepting large payments to authenticate false items."

Stunned, Prentice thought back to the rook's ominous words yesterday.

"Was the thought wisdom that his greed caught up with him? So, he orchestrates the crown theft?"

Dove Haq inclined her head. "The crown is insured. There are also allegations of embezzlement. The crown's insurance payout will more than cover his debts."

"Any truth in the rumor?" Prentice fought to keep doubt from her tone. She hadn't seen the rook in years. Although he'd been pious, she didn't know if he hid behind the authority of the cloth to conceal a dual nature. If he did possess such duplicity, what could cause him to ravage his finances? Gambling? The information both startled and sickened her.

"The Order sent one of the cardinals to review the museum's ledger. I know you're fond of him, Prentice, but money problems, in the extreme, can cause a sense of desperation," Dove Haq said.

"Who reported him?" Prentice asked.

"Zell, the museum archivist. As you can imagine, it has kept a wedge between them. She felt the rook's spending was reckless and his siphoning of museum funds for his own purposes, dishonest."

Prentice found it difficult to believe that behind Rook Renner's ghutra, an evil, greedy man thrived. He wasn't a small-minded person, given easily to the lure of birdsong. It didn't surprise her the vulture reported Rook Renner. She had an air about her of doing whatever it took to get ahead.

"I'll tell you what I find." Prentice left the office.

O nce again, Prentice took the side exit from Dove Haq's office, down the stairs, and landed in the alley. She headed toward one of the university's main streets to grab a carriage to the Sulidae Eagle Station. Once she made a left onto the path that led to the entrance, she heard the stalker's heavy footfalls. *Boots.* No one wore boots this far south.

He'd given himself away without saying a word. The person joined her from the moment she exited. Prentice didn't want to give them any indication that she knew. The individual moved when she did and stopped when she did. An amateur? Maybe. It could be an unafraid bird. At first, the stalker's actions annoyed her. She hoped he'd drop off when she reached the university entrance.

He didn't. It became creepy.

She optioned to keep moving, away from the university. Instead, Prentice walked the trail along the river. As the population thinned, the man became more visible. He abandoned all hints at being incognito. His actions scared her.

She had to get rid of him, so she slowed down to lure him in, allowing the distance between them to close. He didn't stop and she didn't run.

When no one else was around, he approached her from behind. As she stopped abruptly and turned to face him, he growled like a feral animal.

With her talons out, she stood her ground.

He took an aggressive stance.

"Who are you?" she asked, taking in the beige-clad bird with his short-clipped hair and red eyes.

Without warning, he struck her right in the nose, deciding to answer with his fists. Startled, Prentice fired her weapons, but missed. She just saw white.

He hit her again. This time she felt it through her entire body. Prentice used his mass to push off, launching herself into the sky and out of his reach.

"Stop! Who are you?" Prentice shouted, her talons pointed at the offender. "What do you want?" The blood in her left eye turned everything scarlet.

"I'm Ariyo! I want you to back off!" He brandished a short sword. He must've kept the sheath at his back.

"You know I can't and I won't."

"Stay away!" He pointed at her with his weapon.

"No."

"Then, you'll die."

Prentice aimed both talons. "Not tonight."

Before she could fire, Ariyo plunged the sword into his torso.

"No!" Prentice landed a few feet from the dead. She removed her birdcaller from one of her pouches along her utility belt.

Time to get the eagles.

The carriage's creaking wood frame ripped through the early evening quiet. Prentice sat perched on the bench overlooking the river. Her swollen left eye hurt, but she'd steel herself from focusing on it. The attacker hadn't broken her nose, but a hawk with damaged eyes could only use half of their abilities.

When the carriages rolled to a stop, the door to the first one opened, and a woman exited. She wore her hair short-cropped, bore a beautiful set of shiny wings, and a leather holster strapped across her torso. A jagged scar skated down her left eye.

As soon as Prentice saw the wings' golden tips, she cringed.

Galen Gor. Condor.

Condors served as the physical backup for hawks. For The Order, they possessed super strength, excellent sword fighting skills, and could go for long periods of time without food and water.

"Hoot, Prentice," Galen said, with a wave of her

mechanical right arm. She'd lost her original limb in a fight with a rogue earth mage. The Order's blacksmith crafted her a prosthetic with metallic tabs that functioned like a hand so she could still wield a sword.

"What are you doing here? I called for the eagles."

Galen's almond-shaped eye sparkled. Despite being blind in the left eye, she refused to wear a patch. The milky eye served as a badge of her bravery.

"When you called, I was notified, and here I am. The Order deployed me to be the liaison with the Sulidae Eagles."

Prentice got up. "Why hadn't Dove Haq told me?"

"I arrived the day they discovered it missing. Dove Haq may not know I've arrived, but then again she might." Galen shrugged and stretched her wings. "Look, what happened here?"

"You haven't met with the dove?"

"No. Tell me what happened."

Prentice gave her account.

Galen took notes as she talked. Behind them, several eagles evaluated the scene before collecting the body and loading it into the wagon.

"Who is he?" Prentice asked, nodding at the blood spot on the ground where her stalker had been minutes prior.

"Dunno. A nightjar. No identifying papers. We'll run him through to see if we can find an ID tag."

"A nightjar."

"I've had strong feelings they're involved." Galen nodded as she put her notepad in her pouch.

The nightjars' legendary covert skills made them an Order favorite. They used them often for missions that required those skillsets. No wonder Galen started there.

"Come with me," Galen said. "I'll fill you in on the way to the station."

Prentice got in the carriage along with Galen, her mind flashing back to when she saw the condor last. Four years ago, in Lanham, Galen rolled out of their shared dorm, at this very university. They'd shared everything that first year. Birds of a feather, they flocked together all over campus. Prentice traveled to Lanham by train with Galen to start her first day for The Order.

The carriage door closed, and they lunged forward.

Galen said, "There's a lot that's happened. We'll get to those later. I want you to go to medical."

"I'm fine. Tell me what you know."

"Your eye is injured, and your face is battered. I don't want you to put that off."

"Galen, you're not in charge of me, remember." Prentice crossed her arms. She scooted back on the leather seat. "Just tell me. Never mind, I'll read the reports."

"Stubborn as always." Galen looked out the window.

"Don't start," Prentice warned, and looked out her window, too.

Galen became anxious and brooding.

"Our relationship unraveled fast because of that." Prentice turned her attention to Galen.

"You can't sever ties that easily," Galen said.

"Your actions literally tore us apart!"

Galen threw up her hands. "All I said was go to medical. You've been doing this so long and getting away with it, you think you're invincible."

Five years on, Prentice's heart learned to beat again. Galen's leaving created a hole. Even once Prentice got to Lanham, she hadn't seen Galen again until today. The wound opened up, and a lot of the hurt she thought she'd dealt with seeped out in angry, bitter words.

"I don't even like the medical center. What I know of those places is once you enter, you may not come out alive," Galen jeered.

"Fine. I'll go. Now, tell me everything."

Galen began, rubbing the thick scar along her neck. "The nightjars have long been devoted to the goddess's teachings, so much so, the crown would be an ideal relic to steal. The intel we discovered over the last year was they had become zealots, and not the isolating kind, either."

"Really?" Prentice had heard no such thing, but then, the last year, her assignments had been north of Lanham.

"There were two of them on staff. They're renowned for their abilities to blend in, as you know," Galen explained. "Troubled suspicions are eating away at me."

"Sebastian and Pranske, two of the guards."

Galen nodded.

"Why didn't you contact me, tell me you're assigned?" Prentice shifted the conversation.

"News of the theft rippled through the neighborhood. The team has been under a great deal of pressure, as you can imagine. And, I knew you were in Gould," Galen said. She tented her hands in front of her. "I meant to find you, today, but it got away from me."

"Sure. You always enjoyed being the early bird." Prentice winced at the anger in her tone.

Galen spread her hands wide. "It's your case, hawk."

"I want to see all the reports," Prentice said.

"After you go to medical."

"Sure."

Galen grinned, flashing the gap in her teeth.

"You did background on the nightjars."

"Yes, of course. We're doing it on all staff."

"What have you found so far? Start with Pranske."

Galen rubbed her jaw. "He comes across as a mild-mannered gentleman, by all accounts from family and co-workers, but his partners complain of a short temper."

"Physical violence?" Prentice knew his hands had been cut off in the attack. That could be a sign, a message, or a mistake.

Galen leaned back. "I like where you're going with this."

"Galen..."

"Right. Yes. A few skirmishes in local birdbaths, but nothing on campus."

"Did he do any time?" So, the hiring committee knew his history, and they hired him anyway.

Galen took out her notepad again. She flipped through a few pages before stopping.

"Pranske did eighteen months for assaulting several birds three years ago. There were other minor things, but he paid his fines."

The carriage rolled to a stop.

For the second time in as many days, Prentice found herself at the university's entrance.

Galen got out first. "A deal's a deal."

Indeed.

"You need to check-in with the dove. That's the first step in engagement."

Galen shrugged. "It's been busy..."

"As you said."

Galen nodded. "I'll check in tomorrow."

Prentice got out. Her peripheral vision made it a little

harder than she wanted to admit. She navigated the steps in a slow, deliberate manner. Galen left to go talk to the eagles. The other two carriages resumed, heading off to their destination, the eagle station.

Galen shouted up to the carriage driver. "I'll be back."

The vulture nodded. "Yes, sir."

"I don't need an escort." Prentice adjusted her utility belt. "I know the way."

"I do, too," Galen countered.

"You just wanna make sure I go."

"Yes." Galen swept her right hand out. Its gleaming metal caught the sunset's glow. "That's it."

"Fine." Prentice glowered.

Out of all the condors The Order could've assigned, why Galen? The whole situation, already complex, became that much more.

If she didn't know better, she'd say someone at The Order didn't *want* the crown found.

CHAPTER SIX

The horrible news spread through the sleepy university community. Students chirped about it as Prentice walked back to the apartment. When she unlocked the door, she discovered the studio remained as she had left it. Prentice removed her utility belt and placed it on the table. Her gun belt and talons followed. She eased her sore body into the wooden chair, scraping the floor because her arms trembled and failed to lift it. Lanterns lit the room. The round, two-person table bore scars from previous inhabitants.

The apothecary's on-staff doctor had given Prentice a pouch filled with fresh calendula to use three times a day for her injuries.

Prentice removed her headwrap, allowing her long locked hair to fall to her shoulders, and took out a thin-rolled cigarette. Empty and numb, she snapped her fingers for a flame. The Order had taught all hawks some magic to assist with their work. It drew from her blood, her energy, so she didn't do much of it.

As she smoked, she reviewed what she knew. One of the unsettled questions was how the thief got in. It nagged at her. Her mind was a mush of questions and few answers. Hollowed out and uncorked, she closed her eyes and savored the tobacco's flavor. According to her notes, Helena said they swept the museum prior to locking the doors. So no one was left inside afterhours. Galen said they didn't find any signs of forced entry. That meant it had to be an inside job.

Everything pointed to someone who knew the museum.

Outside, thunder rumbled. She rubbed the laceration on her shoulder. The gauze covered the wound, and it itched. The abrasions along her forearms bristled. The doctor applied herbal remedies, and they had dried and crusted over her injuries. Thankfully, she avoided serious head trauma.

"There's nothing beneath the goddess's sky that's certain." Prentice rubbed her temple with one hand. She longed for sweet milk, but the dining hall had closed.

Knocks at the door roused her from her musings. She picked up one of her talons from the table and went to answer it.

"Who's there?" Prentice called.

"Me," Galen replied.

What's she doing here? How did she know this was where I was staying?

Prentice unlocked the door and opened it. The condor swept into the room, carrying a liter glass bottle filled with a creamy liquid.

"I bring sweet milk and information." Galen sat at the table. She set the bottle amongst Prentice's holster and belts. Her metal hand clinked against the glass. "You haven't lost the taste for it. Have you?"

Prentice joined her. "No, I haven't."

"Ah, glasses." Galen hopped up and went to the open shelf of dishware. She took two glasses and returned.

"What are you doing here?" Prentice asked.

Galen smirked. "I thought we could talk."

She uncorked the bottle and poured two feather length of sweet milk into the glasses.

Prentice was parched, so she accepted the drink.

They drank and savored in silence. Almost instantly, Prentice's body aches softened. Sweet milk's healing properties were renowned, but few could stomach it. Hawks thrived on it.

"That's good." Prentice licked her lips.

"More?" Galen asked.

"Please."

Galen topped off both glasses.

"You know what I think?" Galen asked.

Prentice met the condor's amused face. Galen's milky eye glanced up to meet the gaze. "The thief is known to us. They've done it once, twice, and they'd do it again."

"Twice? When?" Prentice perked up.

"There was a theft at the eatery about two weeks prior. Same M.O. No forced entry. Only one item taken."

"What was taken?"

"A pack of ale." Galen smirked.

"That could've been anyone. A thirsty student." Prentice scoffed.

"Think on it, Pren. It was a test run for the museum theft. You'd pick something that wouldn't be missed. Right?"

Prentice didn't think so, but she let Galen talk.

"The theft occurred by one of their own. From their own circle of friends." Galen pounded the table. "No forced entry proved it."

Thunder crashed, rumbling the walls. Galen jumped, her hand on her sword's hilt in a blink.

"I'm outta sorts, too," Prentice said.

"I'm fine. You know, no university is a fortress," Galen remarked. She sipped her sweet milk.

"No, but it's a scandalous idea, an inside job."

Galen's good eye met Prentice's questioning look. "It's dangerous to overlook a dove as a suspect."

"It's not safe to accuse one, either," Prentice said.

"Vultures are circling," Galen warned.

"Vultures hate that saying."

Galen snorted out a laugh.

"What of the rest of the staff?" Prentice drained the rest of her sweet milk. Galen's comments about the dove alarmed her. She removed another cigarette from her pouch. "You want one?"

"Yes!" Galen accepted it.

Prentice took out another. They smoked for several long minutes when Galen brought the conversation back to the theft.

"I suspect all of them," Galen said.

Prentice smiled. Rook Renner had said the same thing. She wanted to get to the truth. Lying was the fastest way to derail an investigation. How many of the staff had lied to her already?

"At first light, I'm going to interview them again, more thoroughly." Prentice blew a stream of smoke through her nose. She needed to dig deeper with them.

Galen snorted. "You want company?"

"Sure."

"The whole staff remains devastated. This will open the wound further."

"Let's start with Sebastian. You like a nightjar for it."

Galen sipped her milk. "For now. I'm not married to it."

Prentice laughed. "The suspect is elusive."

Galen nodded. Her face softened in the lantern light. "You know, I didn't think you'd let me in."

Prentice clucked her tongue. "I don't dwell on the past. I'm forward looking, Galen."

To be honest, Prentice liked having the company. She and Galen rekindling their relationship hadn't been something she thought she needed, but having her friend here helped. Or it could be the sweet milk talking.

Galen smoked. "Good tobacco."

"Thank you," Prentice said. "Got it when I was in Hutchinson Nest. Good growing around the base of the mountains."

Galen raised her eyebrows. "That cost a bit of birdsong."

Prentice nodded. "Indeed."

"How are you feeling?" Galen gave Prentice the once over. "Your eye doesn't look any better. In fact, it looks worse."

"The doctor gave me something for it, but I will heal it myself," Prentice said.

"Do you have enough energy to do so?" Galen took a long drag of the cigarette.

"Yeah." Prentice shrugged. "I haven't used too much."

All hawks' abilities to see the unseen came through their bloodlines, from their mothers. With those skills came their blood magic. Prentice could access her inner cauldron to heal herself, but it took a lot to do so. Thank the goddess, she didn't have too much to repair. No deep cuts or broken bones.

They smoked in silence. Galen poured the last of the sweet milk into both glasses.

"I have further questions for the staff. We need to get them to cooperate."

"People talk to hawks," Galen said.

"Oh, do they? They open up like hungry chicks?"

Galen chuckled. "They do! Your personality puts them at ease. You've closed a lot of cases. You're starting to build a reputation at court."

"Is that so?" Prentice asked. She hadn't been to court enough to know.

Galen blew out a stream of smoke. "Yes. It is."

A fter Galen left, Prentice moved to the bed. Now, full of sweet milk and tobacco, she felt relaxed. She removed her healing kit from one of the pouches on her utility belt. Her body ached and her eye burned; it had been crusted over with fluid and blood. Part of her hated that she hadn't been more prepared for the nightjar's attack.

But the assault happened and lingering on it wouldn't help her discover the thief. Prentice pulled out the metal tin of shea butter balm. Using her thumbs, she worked the lid off and used her index finger to scoop out a tiny bit. *I'll have to refill it soon.* The amount dwindled the more she used it. That would mean a trip home, not to her apartment in Lanham, but to her family home in Tsion Nest.

She spread the shea butter across her nose and then around her left eye, gently massaging it around the puffy parts. Doing so hurt even with the gentlest touches. With her fingernails, Prentice carefully removed the crusty bits clustered at the corners.

She whispered, "*Uponyaji.*"

It stung, but the magic worked in a spray of bright cerulean sparks. Prentice spread her wings wide and lifted up from the bed as the ancestors cradled her in their arms. Their touch didn't cause any additional agony. The cream warmed, and she blew out a long breath as the chorus of her ancestors' songs rose against her ears. Prentice pulled her wings closer, feeling their warmth and softness against her skin. She cleared her mind and started to hum, moving into chanting the chorus. She couldn't see her mothers; her eyes were closed, but she felt their hands beneath her, lifting her from the dredges of pain and agony.

Their words filled the room as she joined in. When they disappeared, Prentice savored the warm embrace of the magical cocoon her magic and wings formed. The healing power pulsated across her skin, the shea butter a conduit and balm across her injuries.

The throbbing power soothed her, and Prentice fell back into its embrace.

CHAPTER SEVEN

Shortly before dawn, Prentice woke in a cold sweat to pounding knocks. She scurried out of bed, but she grabbed one of her talons from the table.

"What?" She cracked the door and peered out.

Galen's eyes were wide, her feathers ruffled in alarm. "The museum's on fire."

A chill skated down Prentice's spine as the words sunk into her sleepy brain. "What?"

"Come on! The fire brigade is already on site, but hurry. Get some clothes on." Galen spun on her heel and walked off distraught.

Hundreds of artifacts are held at the museum. How many priceless items are gone? And why?

Prentice slammed the door closed and hurried to the bathroom. She splashed water on her face, brushed her teeth, and dressed. She pulled on a red dress. It fell to her ankles, and she put on her socks and boots. Sandals wouldn't do if she had to chase a suspect or a fire scene walk-through covered in ash. In moments, she attached her utility and gun belts. She wrapped her hair in its headdress.

She locked her apartment and met Galen at the doors. The condor smoked a cigarette and peered through the haze at Prentice. Already a haze descended on the area, and the acidic scent of burnt items hovered in the air. The stench, shouts, and shrieks of the fire brigade tore through the early morning.

Without speaking, they set off toward the museum about a block away from the faculty housing units. Billowing smoke plumes led them right to the fire. Students and faculty alike had clamored out of bed to witness the blaze. Many wore housecoats and pajamas. Few looked awake.

"Arson is often used in retaliatory ways and to get rid of evidence," Prentice said to Galen.

Galen stretched her wings. "Arson 101."

They reached the scene, where the eagles had used rope to keep the people at bay. Prentice walked up to one of the eagles minding the perimeter.

"Hoot!" the eagle said in greeting. She wore a mask over her mouth. "Careful, hawk. They're still fighting the fire."

"Thank you," Prentice said.

The eagle lifted the rope and allowed Prentice and Galen to enter. They stopped just inside. The ash rained down on them. The heat and intensity forced them to stop. Ahead, firefighters battled the flames belching out of the museum's front doors.

"What do we know so far?" Prentice asked.

Galen dropped her cigarette and ground it out with her boot's heel. She then crossed her arms and sighed.

Prentice watched the water pumped from an enormous container douse the flames in batches. Heavy fire conditions tainted the early morning sky. The firefighters moved fast but also managed to keep the water flow consistent. The fire didn't have time to recover. They drowned it.

Who would do this? Why?

Firefighters scrambled around the scene, seeking a foothold to fight the blaze.

"The fire brigade was contacted approximately fifteen minutes ago about smoke emitting from the museum. They got here in around five minutes. After I got notified, I came up to get you. They've been battling the flames ever since. The eagles are setting up a perimeter around the whole building."

"Who notified you?" Prentice asked.

"Eagle Rick Smathers contacted me after the call came in."

"Who made the call?"

"A student named Avery Stinson." Galen pulled out her notepad and checked. "Yeah."

"Where are they now?"

"In one of the library's study rooms. An eagle is taking his statement."

"Good. I want to talk to Avery, too," Prentice said. The wind hadn't changed, so much of the smoke drifted away from them. Her mouth still tasted like ash and her nostrils burned. She wanted to get out of there, but she wanted to talk to the captain once the fire had been extinguished.

Galen said, "Once it cools, we'll scour the burnt wreckage."

Prentice turned her back to the flames to try to get

sweet air. She glanced over at Galen and said, "It's connected to the crown's theft."

Galen nodded.

"Witnesses to the fire?" Prentice asked.

"The eagles are talking to people now, canvassing the area. Students are in shock and unable to gather their thoughts, and many of them were asleep. We'll take another crack at them later on."

"Going to talk to this Avery Stinson." Prentice left the fire scene and headed toward the library.

Its connection to the museum put it in danger of catching fire. The firefighters had contained the fire because it hadn't reached the library sections of the building. Prentice inhaled a deep breath of non-smoky air as she entered the library via its main doors. The lower level of the university's stacks contained shelves of reference books categorized by the Dodo Decimal system. The upper stacks also followed the same system but held the more popular genres such as fiction and comics. In between stacks, study rooms contained chairs and tables for those looking for quiet or who wanted to engage in group work. When Prentice attended, the soundproof rooms had popular for hanging out and playing games. From the second floor, you could look down to the study tables and chairs in the center of the bottom floor's arrangement. The shelves lined the walls around the rectangular study space. At each of the capacious room's four corners were staircases to the second floor.

Prentice took the closest stairs to the second floor. An eagle stood outside of one of the rooms with his hands hooked into his white uniform's utility belt. He spied

Prentice coming, straightened his back, and put his hands down at his side.

"Hoot, Hawk Tasifa," he said.

"Hoot, er, Eagle…"

"Byrd, sir. I'm Eagle Byrd."

Prentice smiled but didn't laugh. "You're the one who contacted Condor Galen?"

"No, sir. That was my supervisor, Eagle Smathers."

"Hoot. How is our witness?"

"At first, nervous, fidgety. Now, a little more settled, sir," Eagle Byrd said.

"Did you talk to him?" Prentice asked, and he hesitated.

"No, sir, except to explain that he has to remain here until he is given permission to leave."

Prentice wondered if that was all of it. "Did you take his birdcaller?"

"Yes, sir."

"Did he have any other items on his person?"

"No, sir."

"Do you know him?" Prentice asked.

"I…yes, sir, I do," Eagle Byrd said, and his chest fell. "We used to court."

"Oh, okay. Thank you for your honesty. Now, I will ask you again, did you say anything to Avery Stinson about the fire?"

Eagle Byrd's eyes widened. "No, sir. I know my job, and I love it."

Prentice inclined her head. "Thank you."

She pushed by him and went into the room, shutting the door behind her. Seated at the far end of the table, Avery Stinson had his face down on folded arms. When she shut the door, his head snapped up and she was met with the most beautiful eyes, but his hair had been shaved on both sides, leaving a high, electric-blue colored top that he'd picked out to perfection. Around his neck grew a blue beard. Avery Stinson was a Bluejay.

Prentice readied herself. Bluejays were loud, aggressive, and oftentimes bullies.

"Hoot, Avery. I'm Hawk Tasifa." Prentice introduced herself. Now inside, she could smell smoke on her body.

"Hoot, hawk." Avery rubbed his eyes. "How much longer am I gonna be in here?"

"I just have a few questions. Okay?" Prentice took out her notepad and pencil.

"I told Eagle Byrd already."

Prentice sat across from him. "I know. Now, please, tell me. I like to hear it directly from the witness."

Avery rolled his eyes. "Are you serious? It's like what seven? I haven't even been to bed yet. I'm fucking tired."

Aren't we all?

"It won't take long. Start at the beginning." Prentice bit back harsher language. She needed him to talk, not shut down.

Avery sat up, slumped down, and said, "Okay, so I'm returning to campus."

"Where were you coming from?" Prentice asked.

"A house party over in the outer shell."

"What time is this?"

"I dunno. About half an hour ago," Avery said. He scratched behind his ear. "I guess. Can't you get that from the birdcall? I mean, damn."

"Please keep going," Prentice prompted. If she let him get into a rant, she'd have trouble putting him back on the story.

"I could, if you'd quit interrupting with your questions."

Prentice gripped her pencil so hard her knuckles complained.

Avery smirked at her. "Right. So, I came around the corner, heading toward my dorm, when I smelled smoke. First, I thought it was one of those nasty rolled tobacco things, but then, I saw a lot of smoke coming out of the museum's front door. So I called the eagles."

"Did you see anyone or anything suspicious?" Prentice wrote down the limited information he gave her.

"Other than the museum being on fire?"

"Yes." Prentice bit the inside of her cheek to keep from replying with more than one word.

Avery closed his eyes. "Mario asked me that too. The only odd thing was that there was one person outside also, but they didn't seem alarmed by the fire. I figured they were just high or drunk or as sleep-deprived as I was."

"Can you describe this person?" Prentice fought to keep the excitement out of her voice. It might upset or affect Avery's recollection. If she were too eager, the witness could feel obligated and might make up stuff. The opposite could happen too. If she were too eager, the witness could shut down from the pressure. So, Prentice kept her voice even and light.

"Tall, about your height. Wearing a headdress, but not like yours. It was a black ghutra. It caught my eye because black headscarves are rare here. Most are ivory or white or some pattern."

"So, it was a man?" Prentice asked.

Avery opened his eyes and shrugged. "Hell, I dunno. It could've been a thick woman."

"Thank you for your time." Prentice stood up. She put the notepad and pencil away.

"Oh, one more thing," Avery said as he too stood. "The person appeared to be levitating."

Prentice paused. "What?"

Avery laughed. "I could've been whirling, but I could've sworn that big bird was hovering in place. Their feet didn't touch the ground."

Wind magic. Damn it. Who are you?

"Do you think you would recognize them if you saw them again?" Prentice asked.

Avery shook his head. "No. I didn't pay that much attention, honestly. Too fucking tired."

The door burst open. Galen stuck her head in. "Finally found you. Captain wants to see you. Now."

"Thank you, Avery. We'll be in touch." Prentice rushed out of the room. She stopped briefly to tell Eagle Byrd, "Avery's free to go."

She and Galen hurried down the stairwell, out of the library, and over to the museum. The fire had been put out and blackened remains smoldered. Most of the crowd had gone back inside.

Prentice and Galen ducked under the ropes and headed over to the captain. She met them halfway. Ash framed her face where her goggles had been. Her jet-black hair had been tied behind her in a low ponytail. The yellow fire-retardant coat collar had been turned up. It bore ash and debris.

"Hoot, hawk. I'm Captain Allison Charlesworth," the captain said. She wiped her face. "The fire moved with terrifying speed. It melted paint off the doors, and it burned a large section of the rook's office. They cleared the area. Fire's out."

"Are you thinking arson?" Prentice asked.

"Oh yes. Accelerant splashes all over the areas we could spot because they're cool enough. There are pour patterns from the courtyard through the museum doorway and into the inner room. It reeks of lantern oil and is consistent with how fast the fire grew," Captain Charlesworth said.

"Can we look through it?" Prentice asked.

"It's still pretty hot in areas, hawk. I don't recommend it," Captain Charlesworth said.

Just then, a young firefighter burst through a group of firefighters clearing the area.

"Captain Charlesworth! Come quick!" he managed, eyes wide as saucers. "We found something."

Prentice moved. "Lead the way. Now!"

Captain Charlesworth jerked out of her pause and followed.

The firefighter nodded and went back into the museum through what used to be the front doors. The odor hit Prentice just as she crossed the threshold. Acidic and thick with smoke, each breath contained ash and death.

"Stay here!" Captain Charlesworth put her mask back on.

Prentice removed a piece of cloth from her utility belt and held it to her nose. "Smoke."

"Yeah." Galen nodded and did the same. She kept her eyes ahead as they followed Captain Charlesworth toward Rook Renner's office.

Outside of Rook Renner's office door, the young firefighter stood.

"Hawk Tasifa," Prentice introduced herself.

He nodded. "It's bad in there."

"Thanks for the warning," Prentice said and entered the remnants of the rook's office.

"I told you two to wait," Captain Charlesworth snapped.

"I'm a hawk, captain. I have to see with my own eyes," Prentice said. "It looks like a violent struggled occurred here. The fire spared most of the outer edges of the back wall."

"Not all was spared," Galen said, directing Prentice's attention to the floor.

In a fetal position, a blackened body gave off smoke tendrils.

"Now, we officially have a depraved killer on our hands." Galen raised her hands.

"Who is it?" Captain Charlesworth asked.

"Dunno." Galen shrugged. "Nothing of value appears to be taken or irreplaceable."

"This person's life, Galen," Prentice said.

"Right."

"We will need a doctor to go over the body. Galen, go over to medical or ask the eagles for their coroner and the coffin carriage."

"Sure." Galen winked her good eye at Captain Charlesworth and left.

"You suspect foul play?" Captain Charlesworth asked.

"Yes, I do," Prentice said. "Is it safe for me to look around?"

"Yes, just watch where you step. Water can loosen places in the floor where its pooled."

"Thank you."

Prentice closed her eyes and pulled deep from within,

engaging her hawk sight. When she opened her eyes, everything was larger, closer. She didn't have to bend down to the body. The torso had been on fire the longest. Extensive burning of the body. Good thing, for the burnt stench of flesh hit her hard, and she coughed to dislodge it from her mouth.

There!

The right clutched hand held a piece of scorched parchment. Prentice took tweezers from her utility belt along with an envelope. She removed it from the person's blackened fist and deposited it into the envelope. She put both the tweezers and the clue inside two different pouches.

Next, the fluttering hum drew her attention to an open book, placed on the far corner of the desk, inches from being burned as most of the desk had been consumed by flames. The book's pages flapped in a fan's breeze. The fan had been placed in the window and an early morning breeze turned its blades.

The book was a ledger, the museum's, from the looks of it. She spied various fingerprints along the pages' edges. Some were the rooks. She knew this from the minute flecks of chocolate and olive oil in the prints. The others were Killion's. Her faint scent infused those prints, and Prentice saw the metal bits from her earrings along the prints. Killion must have rubbed some of the metal's paint onto her finger when putting them on and with sweat transferred them to the ledger. Beneath the thick odor of ash and water, Killion's perfume remained.

Why was Killion looking over the ledger? With whom?

From a quick scan of the figures, Prentice noticed the museum had a surplus, not a deficit.

Why had Zell lied? Did it put Killion in an early grave?

Prentice stepped back from the desk and drank in the debris and smoldering damage. There, sticking out from underneath a pile of blackened parchment, a discarded glove. Prentice removed her tweezers again and picked it up. It was too large for one of her envelopes, so she used the tweezers to make it as small as it could go. Then she stuffed it into an empty pouch. She couldn't close it, but she had another clue. Along the walls, red stains covered some of the books not torched—blood spatter. Still more smoke coming out of various places in the bookshelves.

"The doctor's on her way with a recover unit," Galen said as she stepped into the office. "I see you're in your power."

Prentice didn't answer. Galen being an obvious bird didn't warrant a response.

"Who is this?" Galen asked.

"Killion."

"How did she end up like this?"

"I dunno, yet. I'm still processing the scene, but if she came in here to subvert justice, she sealed her fate."

Galen looked around "She didn't burn herself up."

Prentice scanned the ceiling. "No, she didn't. Someone laid in ambush for her. One thing I do know is that this was about destruction. A destruction of property and evidence."

"Can you conjure the last visitors?" Galen asked, referring to hawks' ability to conjure the last few moments that occurred in a space.

"No, the fire has damaged the essence. Between the blaze and the water, it's gone. I can't conjure it to view."

"Damn," Galen swore. "It's like this person is one step

ahead of us. Who knows all the things hawks can do? That
nightjar deliberately attacked your eyes."

Prentice closed her eyes, took in a deep breath to slowly
end her hawk abilities. She'd seen all she could with those
eyes. Now, the darkness would come for goddess knew
how long. Each time she used her hawk abilities to see the
unseen, her human eyes would take longer to recover, until
one day, like her mother and grandmother and mothers
before, Prentice would go blind.

"It does feel like someone is cunning and connected to
court," Prentice said, whispering this last so that only
Galen heard her.

"Where did the captain go?" Galen asked.

Prentice opened her eyes, but as before, she saw only
darkened shadows. "I dunno."

"Are you done here?" Galen asked. "You're done. The
glow's gone from your eyes."

"Yeah. I've seen enough," Prentice said, and stuck out
her hand. "Galen…"

She couldn't see Galen's face clearly, only a dark,
shadowy blob. The warm metal of Galen's hand grabbed
her hand.

"It's happening already," Galen stated with a hint of
sadness.

"It started the first time I invoked my hawk eyes, Galen.
You know how this goes," Prentice said. "Don't pity me."

"Let's go." Galen held her arm and guided her back
through the burnt-out museum debris and out into the still
early morning sunlight.

"I reek of smoke." Prentice winced at the odor.
Whenever her eyesight dimmed, her other senses increased
in compensation. "I'm heading back to the apartment."

"Okay." Galen gripped her arm and added, "Me too."

As they exited, a herd of duck reporters flocked around them.

"Can you tell us about the theft, hawk?" the duck quacked, pushing the others out of the way.

"No comment," Prentice said, and gripped Galen's hand tight. She could just make out a sea of white-clad ducks, all huddling around her, encroaching into her personal space.

Galen pushed through the throng, before unsheathing her sword. Prentice didn't see it, but she heard it. Gasps and more quacking of questions until the smooth, calming sound of Dove Haq's voice drew them to her, like, well, ducks to water.

"Sorry about that," Galen said as she led Prentice away from the dove's voice.

"They act like a bunch of vultures," Prentice said.

"The vultures probably hate that saying too." Galen laughed.

CHAPTER EIGHT

Hours later and back in the apartment, Galen held up a basket.

"Lunch?"

"That smells delicious! Yes," Prentice said.

Galen put a glass jar, foggy from steam, on the table. She removed a cloth-covered, wooden bowl and a smaller, square bottle, and uncorked it.

"Salad dressing." Galen passed it to Prentice.

Prentice sat at the table in her fresh, clean clothes. She'd bathed and washed off the grime and smoke smell. She wore her hair up in a towel and put on her official scarlet hawk dress and boots. The Order's insignia lay at the center of the dress, just above her cleavage. Her belts lay on her bed, leaving the table clear for an early lunch or late breakfast. Her sight had returned and so had her appetite.

Prentice looked up at Galen. "What did the raven find?"

"Killion had a scarf stuffed down her throat. It

suffocated her. The body was burned after she died. Probably an attempt to get rid of evidence."

"A scarf. What kind?"

"One usually used for a headwrap, black. It's too common to trace. It's every student's favorite accessory this summer."

"Did she give it to you?"

"Yes."

Prentice nodded. "Leave it with me."

Galen placed the bowl with bag containing the scarf on the floor beside the table.

"Did you get plates?" Prentice got up to go to the dishware shelves.

"No."

"Do I smell fish?" She got two plates and returned to the table.

"Yes, for you." Galen pushed the bowl toward her. "It's in the salad."

"Aren't you eating?" Prentice returned to the table and removed the damp cloth to reveal a delicious trout salad.

"I'll have the milk." Galen sat across from her. "You enjoy."

"Galen..."

"You know condors can go for days without food. But I will take one of your cigarettes."

Prentice got up, went to her utility belt, took out a cigarette, and passed it to Galen, who lit it with her own lighter, embedded in her mechanical hand.

Prentice ate. "Let's go through it."

"Someone steals the Five-Feathered Crown, injures the guards, and used wind magic."

"Which is forbidden," Prentice noted, and forked lettuce into her mouth.

"You're warned off the case by a nightjar."

Prentice nodded. "Someone torched the museum and killed Killion."

"Why?" Galen asked aloud.

"Is it connected?"

"How can it not be?" Galen flexed her arm.

"That was rhetorical."

As Prentice ate, Galen removed small vials and a few tools from her utility belt. She began working on her hand.

"I need more clues," Prentice said. "We're missing something."

"Who's left?" Galen winced as she screwed a nut tighter.

"The nightjar guards, Zell, Helena."

"You know, when we compete for resources, we become animals."

"We *are* animals," Prentice said.

"True."

"The nightjars couldn't have done the arson," Prentice explained. "Pranske is still in a magic-induced coma, Helena was in medical, and Sebastian would most likely be asleep."

"We need to confirm his whereabouts."

"That leaves Zell and Rook Renner."

"I'll get those times nailed down for each of them." Prentice drank more water. "If they don't have alibis, they're a suspect."

"There's no proof that the arson is connected."

"No, but I don't believe in coincidence. And we have the glove," Prentice said.

"Glove?" Galen looked up from her tinkering.

"I found a glove underneath the body."

"Let's see what we find," Galen said.

"I'm going to dowse to identify this glove to see who it belonged to," Prentice said.

Prentice recounted what she found at the wreckage of Rook Renner's office.

"What's on the parchment?" Galen asked.

"I dunno." Prentice put down her fork and went to her utility belt. She took out the envelope and returned to the table.

Galen cleared away the used dishes and containers. Prentice pushed her salad aside. She placed the parchment on the table and gently unrolled it. Parts of it had been burned away.

---

arrive at so much damage to the goddess. You will pay for your dishonor.

~ Achiel

"Achiel?" Galen frowned.

"It means 'one' in the old speech," Prentice explained. "This is definitely a threat, but was it to Killion or Rook Renner?"

"Good question." Galen began replacing the vials back into her pouch.

Prentice replaced the parchment into the envelope and resumed eating her salad.

Galen picked up the cigarette, relit it, and smoked.

"Could an act of kindness have been repaid with venom?" Prentice asked.

"Yeah. Happens all the time." Galen got up and started pacing.

"You know, in many cases we can't answer the why, but I feel that is the crux to finding the crown, the culprit, and the murderer."

Galen nodded as she walked.

"I could smell death. I knew someone had died before I went inside the office, even with all the smoke," Prentice said.

"Let it out," Galen encouraged.

"Each of these assignments are mentally and physically exhausting, but it sticks with me. It will for the rest of my life." Prentice finished her salad. She drank the water Galen brought from the dining hall.

"Yeah, so next steps?" Galen asked.

"I'm going to dowse these objects and then go interview Zell," Prentice answered.

"Yes, sir." Galen collected her things. "Meet you for dinner?"

"Sure. Meet you back here."

Galen left.

Prentice cleared the rest of the dishes from the table, stacking them inside the sink. She'd clean up later. Time rushed away from her, and she had much to do.

She washed her hands, dried them on a towel, and returned to her utility belt. The first thing she removed was a piece of folded parchment. She used clean glasses and teacups to hold down the four corners. Next, Prentice took out a pencil from another pouch and walked over to the table. On the parchment, she drew a circle and divided it into six equal slices. She labeled the sections with the names of each suspect.

Zell, Killion, Sebastian, Pranske, Helena, and Renner

Next, Prentice went to a different pouch on her utility belt and removed her dowsing pendulum. It featured a hawk that rested at the end of a silver chain. Prentice removed her pen dagger from its sheath on her utility belt. It bit into her index finger, and she wiped the blood across the casting stone's talons.

She whispered, *"Determiner."*

The blood magic invoked in a spray of blue sparks. Prentice held it over the glove she discovered in the rook's office wreckage. She counted to ten and remained still as the pendulum gained momentum. It swung above the names on the parchment in an arc, propelled by her blood magic. She continued to chant the incantation. The apartment bled away, leaving only herself and the parchment. The pendulum swirled faster and faster until it blurred.

Then as soon as Prentice thought it would shoot out of her fingers, it slowed until it settled on the name.

Renner

"By the goddess!" Prentice blinked and stood up. The glove belonged to Rook Renner. That didn't move her anywhere closer to solving this case and finding the crown. The glove was in his office. Finding it proved nothing.

Next, she took the scarf Galen said was stuffed into Killion's throat. Again, Prentice invoked the incantation, and again, the pendulum swirled. The silver hawk flew around and around, until it settled on a name.

Killion

Prentice snapped her fingers, igniting a small flame to which she cleaned the pendulum, running the silver hawk over the fire. Prentice laid it on the table to cool while she folded the parchment and returned it to its utility pouch. She put the scarf back in its container. After cleaning her pen dagger, she returned it to its sheath, and her pencil to its pouch and notepad. The dowsing pendulum went back into its velvet pouch, too.

What a complete waste of time.

Annoyed, she attached her utility belt and gun belt to her waist and set out to find something meatier than what her magic provided.

Outside, the noonday sun hadn't rid the area of the smoky film from the morning's fire. Prentice shook her wings. Although she bathed and changed clothes, she couldn't shake the layer of dread and the film of death.

She took the side entrance up to the dove's office. After the arson, she had to meet with Dove Haq and update her on what she'd found and to discuss the attack on the museum. Due to the way things occurred, Prentice didn't get to her until now. No doubt the dove would be furious.

Prentice entered via the side door and found the foot traffic had increased. With the front of the museum guarded by eagles as an active investigation scene, the hallway that led into the building and connected the museum, the library, and the dove's office had been closed.

She made it to the second floor, walked down the short corridor and into the dove's office. Cooler than the hall, the long rectangular room had the windows pushed up, and breezes swept through the space. She found the secretary, Paige, a round hen with dull hair, glasses perched on her beak, and ruddy cheeks. She had an amazing laugh.

"Hoot, Hawk Tasifa. Dove Haq is expecting you, was expecting you hours ago."

"I apologize."

"Oh, no." The hen cut Prentice a sharp look. "I don't want or need your apology. She does."

She jutted her thumb at the closed door behind her.

Prentice said, "Well, I'm here now. May I go in?"

"Yes."

Prentice approached the door that led to the dove's anteroom. She had been briefed on the staff just yesterday in this very room, and now, one of those individuals was dead. She rapped on the door with her heart inching into her throat.

"Come," Dove Haq's velvety voice called.

Prentice turned the knob and entered to find the dove seated in an overstuffed chair with a book opened on her lap. She looked up at Prentice but didn't smile. Her elegant visage tilted up to look over Prentice, and with a sweep of her hand, she told Prentice to sit.

With a strong sense of foreboding tightening her stomach into a knot, Prentice eased down into the neighboring chair. The anteroom held art from the Chicken Scratch Period of vibrant colors and bold strokes that spoke of chaos and order, madness and sanity, or so those who studied that era of art proclaimed. The Chicken Scratch Era encompassed the period of fifteen years before Owl Nadiya. Chickens broke out in artistic favor with their scratches. Prentice couldn't tell what the art was supposed to convey, but perhaps she didn't have the right eye.

"So, while you and the condor have flapped around

doing nothing, someone burned my museum, very nearly to the ground. I don't want excuses, Prentice, I want answers. Where is the Five-Feathered Crown? Why is one of my staff dead, and who burned down my museum!?"

Prentice jumped at the escalation in volume. Dove Haq's expression hadn't changed despite the volume and acidity of her voice.

"I need to continue interrogating the staff. My working theory is that the theft was done in conjunction with someone on the inside, someone with a working knowledge of the museum."

The dove sat back in her seat, her grip on the chair's arm relaxed, and she tented her long fingers in front of her.

"Someone on the inside. Why?"

"There wasn't any forced entry, and the guards didn't leave anyone lingering in the museum after it closed. That meant someone had to either let the thief in or allowed them to remain inside after closing."

Dove Haq pressed her lips together.

Prentice continued. "As for the fire, it was meant to cover up evidence. Of what, I'm still looking into it. It is still early days, dove, but we are making progress, albeit slowly."

"I don't have time for slow. All of Aves is demanding to know the crown's location. Reporters are landing in Sulidae as we speak. I'm the laughingstock at court. I don't think I need to explicitly explain how much this needs to be wrapped up. Soon."

"No, sir. I am working as fast as I can. I also need the addresses for the remaining staff. I want to do another round of interrogations."

"I'll get my secretary, Paige, to call them. You're going direct from here?"

"Yes."

Dove Haq made a note in her open book in her lap. She wrote a few things, and then stood. "Is that all?"

"Yes. I'll report in when I find out more," Prentice said.

Dove Haq said, "Be sure you do. Daily."

"I am sorry for your loss."

"I have to contact her family and then respond to the students and faculty. You have no idea what an instructor's death does to a university, especially one like this." Dove Haq led me through the door and out again to the office.

"Paige, give Hawk Tasifa the addresses she needs."

Prentice decided to start with Zell. She lived on campus and was the closest. Rook Renner had relocated to working in one of the library study rooms.

She'd start with the two of them and then move out to the other staff members not in the hospital.

The heat from the crown's missing theft put the glare on Prentice, as if someone had a large magnifying glass. She headed down the stairs and out into the too-hot sun with her mind full of questions that needed answer. The only way to get to the bottom of things was to rattle the birdcages.

CHAPTER NINE

Prentice walked into one of the library's study rooms to find Rook Renner bent over yellowed parchment, his pipe tight in his teeth.

"Hawk Tasifa," he greeted her over his shoulder.

"I have a few questions," Prentice said.

She took a seat across from him in the hard, wooden chair. Unlike the ones in her apartment, they didn't have cushions.

"You heard about Killion." Prentice didn't ask it as a question. For one of his colleagues to be found dead in his office and in such a horrific manner, she expected more emotion, questions, *something* more than the apathy the rook presented.

"Yes, may the goddess embrace her." Rook Renner's thick fingers drifted across what Prentice could make out as a map.

She watched him. He held the same indifferent expression he always wore. Was it an apathy toward life itself or a greater love for research and the goddess? At court, some proclaimed that Rook Renner had the best bird brain in all of the kingdom. She didn't know the rook well enough to know for sure. Rooks were social, but they enjoyed their academic cliques and groupings.

"Tell me about her. Do you know why she was in your office after hours?" Prentice asked, taking out her notepad and pencil and ready to begin the interview in earnest.

"Killion started out righteous, but she became a bit of a sinner." Rook Renner stroked his beard.

"Meaning?" Prentice asked.

"She held Sebastian in her thrall, you know. It all started innocent enough, but here lately, she had come to pull his strings," Renner said.

"You allowed that to continue?" Prentice sat up and met his gaze. It didn't feel right. Why would he allow an unprofessional relationship to begin and then reject it?

The rook shrugged. "It made sense they could connect, colleagues do. It was a very secret relationship, and at first, I didn't interfere. Lately Killion became predatory with him."

Prentice fought to keep her face neutral. She'd eaten lunch with Killion, and she spied nothing of the kind. Perhaps she was different with Sebastian or in the workplace.

"What did you do?" Prentice looked back to her pad.

He sighed. "I talked to her. Coached her to sever her relationship with him."

"What did she say?"

Had Sebastian killed Killion out of anger at being rejected?

"She agreed. She said it had gotten out of hand, and she ended it a few days before the theft." Renner turned his attention to the map.

"Why was Killion in your office?" Prenticed asked again.

Rook Renner mumbled to himself and adjusted the antique map.

"I know you were there with her. Your residue remains," Prentice bluffed.

The rook didn't turn around. "Fire dissolves spiritual ether."

"True, but we have other evidence." Prentice pivoted.

His beady, dark eyes shifted to her.

"Bloody hawk. You'll find out eventually. Killion and I were reviewing this year's ledger and inventory. Dove Haq suspects embezzlement. The Order has sent their bookkeepers. They already have the previous five years' ledger."

Prentice sat back in the uncomfortable chair.

"Did Killion steal the crown?"

Rook Renner sighed. "I don't know, but as I've said before, anyone could have done it with the proper motivation."

"Like mounting debts," Prentice said.

He raised his thick, bushy eyebrows and chuckled. "That took longer than I thought. I wondered when you get the courage to ask me."

"I'm asking now." Prentice didn't join him in mirth. This was serious.

"Calm your feathers. I'm short on birdsong due to a string of misfortunes I won't recount now, but know this, young hawk, I would never sacrifice or sell my reputation, this university's reputation, or the goddess's treasures. Not if my life depended on it. To a degree, it does. This is my life's work, and someone is doing their best to discredit and destroy it." Rook Renner shook his fist at her, caught himself, and settled back in the chair. Once he collected himself, he returned his attention to the map.

"So, the crown's theft, the fire, and Killion's slaying are all about you?" Prentice had never seen the rook so animated.

"It seems that way. Doesn't it?" Rook Renner said.

To her surprise, she agreed. "It does look that way. Why would anyone want to harm you?"

The rook sighed heavily. "I have no idea."

"So, no idea who?"

"If I did, I would resolve this already, young hawk."

You are not making this easy, rook.

"Where were you this morning between 5 a.m. and 7 a.m.?" Prentice asked.

The rook said, "In chapel, praying to the goddess. Dove Haq will confirm my presence there."

"Thank you for your time," Prentice said and left the study room.

As she walked, she put her notepad and pencil in her utility belt. Students from various flocks sat perched on seats, talking, studying, and enjoying the cooler temperatures and access to the books and resources.

Prentice exited into the simmering afternoon Sulidae sun. Zell couldn't work at the museum and had been displaced like Rook Renner; however, she didn't keep an office at the museum, but rather had an office in the Antiquities department. Prentice headed toward the opposite side of campus, but after not finding her there, headed toward Zell's home.

The University of Sulidae was one of the leading spiritual and educational centers in the Kingdom of Aves. Its architecture reflected the ancient building structure of

The Order and later the Edmonton nesters. The goddess's chapel had been erected first and so it functioned as the center or heart of campus. The other buildings spiraled out, like spokes on a wheel.

Over the years, various doves had further repaired, renovated, and extended the campus beyond its initial span. The afternoon sun flushed against blue sky and spied through palm trees as Prentice made her way to the opposite end of the campus. This section had been the oldest. Rooks held tenure and devoted their lives to their subjects. Professors worked for a wage and had to pay for their housing and meals. Both Zell and her partner were professors. Of course, on-campus housing cost less than living in the egg or outer shell. The faculty townhomes were converted from an abbey. It once housed those who served in the goddess's chapel. These residences sat on top of a small hill. Prentice leaned into the incline, but it wasn't too difficult. It wasn't like the mountains and hills in Gould.

Once she reached the complex, she stood in awe. Despite its age, these buildings were beautiful. Decorated in carved stucco, the round windows looked out onto the campus down the hill. Exterior decorations displayed arch spandrels and window panels, consisting of scrolling and meandering vines ending in half palmettes. A flat roof was carried by slender columns connected by four arches. Triangular shaped battlements adorned the top of the walls.

Above each door sat a hand-painted number in gorgeous calligraphy.

Prentice walked beneath the canopy strung above the doorways until she came to number four. She knocked.

"Yes?" Zell called from the other side.

"It's me. Hawk Tasifa. Dove Haq said she'd call," Prentice said.

Prentice heard locks and chains moments before the door cracked open. Zell peered out at her, and then opened the door wide.

"Yes, she did. Come in." Zell stepped back from the door and waved her inside.

Prentice entered the cool, lavender-scented home. Lit candles flickered as breezes slipped through the square, small room. The front door emptied into a short hallway, which split into the living room on the left, and to the right, a kitchen. Ahead, Zell gestured to the sofa, a light purple chaise and a matching loveseat decorated with ivory pillows. An ornate rug, woven no doubt in the Glassberg Nest, covered most of the living room floor. It held flecks of gold that caught the sunbeams. The furniture was positioned in an L-shaped pattern around a wooden coffee table. A teacup rested on the table, sending steam into the air. Rolls of parchment covered the chaise.

Zell cleared some of the items away and swept her hand at the loveseat. She wore a long, ivory linen dress and sandals. Her gray skin shone as if oiled; her hair had been braided into one single plait and coiled on top of her head. Long, silver earrings dangled from her ears, and a thick silver necklace with a square piece of silver-framed turquoise completed her outfit. Her makeup remained as it had the first time Prentice met her.

"Please sit. Do you need anything to drink? Eat?" Zell asked.

"No, thank you. I had lunch already." Prentice sat perched on the edge of the loveseat. She removed her notepad and pencil, adjusted her position.

"So, what do you want?" Zell crossed her legs and tried to look relaxed.

Why is she so uneasy?

"I have a few questions about the crown theft and about the museum's arson," Prentice said.

Zell looked at Prentice but didn't comment.

"Why did you report Rook Renner to Dove Haq about possible embezzling?" Prentice decided to go direct to the one question burning the brightest.

Zell didn't flinch. "He is stealing from the museum."

"How did you find out?" Prentice kicked herself for not phrasing the question better. "You're an archivist. Reviewing the ledger isn't in your duties, so how did you know or believe the rook was stealing?"

"Well, there were several quality artifacts that came in from Tsion. Rook Renner refused to purchase them, citing lack of funds. But we had completed a fundraiser only three days before."

"He could've rejected those items because they weren't genuine artifacts," Prentice said.

Zell's answer was flimsy as wet parchment.

"Tell me you had more than a hunch that the director of the Goddess museum renowned throughout all of Aves was a thief. Something tangible that you risked his reputation."

Prentice couldn't believe it. *The gall!*

The vulture rubbed her hands on her dress. "Now hang on, hawk. I'm not some vindictive bird. Someone told me the rook was stealing."

"So, hearsay," Prentice said.

"It was a reliable source," Zell countered.

"If that's true, why didn't they go to the dove?"

Zell hung her head.

"I know when I've been lied to. I see the unseen, Zell," Prentice pressed.

The professor closed her arms and huffed. "Killion told me."

"How did *she* know?"

Zell remained tight-lipped.

"You just took her word for it."

There had to be more than *this*.

Zell shrugged. "Maybe ask Sebastian or Killion."

"Why Sebastian?"

"He's Killion's partner, or he was."

"Tell me about that." Prentice put her pencil down and gave Zell her full attention.

"About what? Their relationship?"

"Sure."

"Why would you want to know about them?" Zell asked.

"The goddess's crown is missing. The Order will tear through Aves to find it. The museum housing her treasures has been burned down. All secrets will be laid bare. Reporters are already circling. They will peck it out." Prentice bit the inside of her cheek at losing her patience. Zell's stonewalling wouldn't get her the information she needed.

Zell popped up from the chaise. She walked to the patio doors and looked out.

"Look, she didn't talk to me about him. Believe it or not, we had work to do and discuss." Zell sighed.

Prentice ignored Zell's snap. No one enjoyed other people prying open their closets and rummaging inside. She inclined her head for Zell to continue. Thick candles flickered in the occasional breeze. It swept through parted windows.

The quiet grew heavy. After several minutes, Zell cracked beneath its weight.

She turned to face Prentice. "A few times she spoke about Sebastian's connection to Pranske. It concerned her."

"Why?"

"I don't know. Look, I truly do not know. She never said. When I asked her, she would just say it was complicated."

"Pranske and Sebastian are like brothers. Yes?"

Zell laughed. "There's no love between them. Truth is, hawk, there was a lot of hate and discontent in that family. Sebastian used her grief to get them together. Birds flocked like that."

"What did Killion grieve about?"

Zell paused. "You really don't see everything. Do you?"

Prentice didn't say anything.

"Killion's twin sister was slain, maybe two years ago. The eagles didn't discover the person who did it. This worked a darkness, a sadness and whatnot for her. Sebastian lost a sibling too. They became close."

"Why didn't you mention this before?" Prentice noted Zell's slickness for deflection.

Did Zell harbor jealousy and resentment? Yes, was it enough for Zell to kill Killion?

"Their friendship turned into something ugly." Zell shrugged.

"Go on."

Zell's wide eyes rolled. "You're going to have to find that for yourself. Maybe ask them."

Prentice nodded. "I will. Is there anything else?"

"Such as?"

"Where were you at five this morning?" Prentice looked up from her notepad.

"Here, asleep."

"Anyone verify that?"

Zell smirked. "No. Nadia works early. She left around four."

"Thank you." Prentice got up.

Zell followed Prentice to the door. "You suspect me of stealing the crown and burning down the museum?"

"Right now, everyone's a suspect, but not just for arson, for slaying."

Zell gasped. "What? Who's dead?"

"Haven't you heard? Killion is dead." Prentice watched Zell's response.

The vulture stumbled. "Killie is dead."

That's a new nickname. I hadn't heard that one before. So, Zell and Killion were friends. Frenemies?

"Yes."

Zell hugged herself and turned back toward the living room sofa. She sank into the seat and put her head in her hands.

"Do you know someone who would want to harm Killion?" Prentice asked.

Zell's big, luminous eyes blinked, and tears spilled over. "Now that you mentioned it."

"Who?"

"Um, Sebastian. They were lovers, and um, I know Killie ended it. Rook Renner discovered the relationship."

Was Sebastian harboring some deep-seeded hunger for revenge?

"Anyone else?"

Zell shrugged. "I don't know. She didn't have many friends, and she kept to herself most of the time."

Now that she knew Killion had died, information flowed, no hesitation but many details.

"Sebastian was great friends with Pranske. In fact, it was Sebastian who recommended him to the rook for a job. But once Pranske found out about the relationship, Killion was an ostrich, he exploded. She told me that Pranske had cornered her at work and threatened her."

"When did this happen?" Prentice quirked an eyebrow.

Zell bit her lower lip in thought. Then she sighed. "Last week, a few days before the crown was stolen."

"When did she end the relationship with Sebastian?"

Zell huffed. "That same day Pranske threatened her. She said it wasn't worth both Rook Renner and Pranske forcing her to end things. Besides, she wasn't that into it anyway. So, she broke it off."

Prentice said, "Thank you. I'm sorry for your loss."

"Get that damn *pigeon*." Zell wiped her eyes and balled her hands into fists. She bounced them against her thighs. "Don't let him get away with this."

Prentice met her eyes. "I will."

CHAPTER TEN

Prentice hailed a carriage at the university's entrance. The horse's hoofbeats provided a song to her travels. As she looked out the window, she pondered Zell's words. There was a conspiracy afoot. But why? For what reasons did stealing the crown and murder have? Who benefitted?

Killion's death put Prentice behind the curve. She'd lost a piece of the puzzle by not interrogating the instructor further at lunch. At first, Prentice thought the slaying had been a byproduct of the museum's fire. Now, after speaking with Zell, she figured Killion had been targeted.

Beyond the university's gates, the Sulidae Egg appeared like a mirage in the desert, a shimmering jewel in the sand. The beige-coated landscape extended as far as her eyes could see. Lush green palm trees dotted the street corners like emeralds along the sidewalks. Colorful awnings soared and rippled in the breeze above the shops' doorways. A series of cool currents scented the area with river water's earthiness. The merchants' buildings and open-air markets gave way to alcoves of residential neighborhoods. Camels, horses, carriages, and bicycles vied for road space, and Prentice's ride stopped often. Flat, timber houses with thatched roofs and colorful rugs welcomed guests. Each home resembled its neighbor. This area lined the outer shell on the other side of a low mud-brick wall.

The horse's clopping stopped. It whinnied their arrival.

Prentice knew from her time at university that the Nightendale community used to be an old railroad hub before a newer one, closer to the school, had been built. The homeowners fled to other communities along the railroad line. In the wake of the mass exodus, nightjars moved in and had resided here ever since, four decades ago now. They'd turned it into a religious section of the egg. The streets were empty all day and the chapels full all night.

Sebastian and Pranske resided here.

Zell, Rook Renner, Sebastian, Pranske, and Helena.

Within this group someone orchestrated a slaying and a theft. She was missing something. Prentice climbed out of the carriage and paid the driver his birdsong.

"Can you wait here for me?" she asked the vulture.

"Yes. It will cost you," he replied through the cloth mask and head covering, beige like his head to foot covering, which was cinched around the waist with a brown leather belt.

"I understand," Prentice said.

She approached Sebastian's single-story home. It looked like all the others in this block. A bicycle lay flat against the building, and a scarlet number served to differentiate his home from the others. She knocked on the door and it opened.

"Sebastian?" Prentice put her hand on her talon.

No response.

She inched further into the shadowy room. "Sebastian. It's Hawk Tasifa. Paige called."

Lanterns flickered and rested along various surfaces around the room. The dirt floor had been covered with rugs. Two pair of sandals had been placed on a black mat inside the entranceway. She didn't see them at first, but now her vision had adjusted to the low light. She didn't want to use her hawk abilities.

"Sebastian?"

Prentice's feathers rose at the possibility of danger. She pulled both talons from their holster and used them to slice through the gloominess as she made her way to the next, smaller room.

The door had been opened a crack. As she got closer, a series of deep snores made her relax.

When she got into the room, she spied drinking vessels scattered around the bed. Sebastian slept on a feathered mattress on the floor. Plants lined the room's outer perimeter around the bed. Nature and drink collided in the tiny space. It reeked of ale and sweat.

Prentice put away her talons, walked over to Sebastian, and bent down beside him.

Sebastian jerked awake.

"Bad dreams or worse, a memory?" Prentice relocated to the end of his bed and out of his reach.

"Neither." He put on his turban. "What are you doing here?

"I have follow-up questions."

"About what? I told you everything I know." His words sounded full of sleep.

"About Pranske." Prentice studied him. "You been drinking?"

"Yeah." He rubbed his eyes.

He smelled like he was still drinking.

"A brother knows another," Prentice pointed out.

He sat up, conflicting emotions playing on his face. "I'm not answering your questions."

"All questions are answered in time. I'm a hawk, Sebastian. I will find out. I'd rather hear it from you." Prentice crossed her arms. "You know more than you're telling me."

"No, I don't."

Prentice increased her pressure. "I will rip your life apart. I will dig until everything you have ever done is laid bare. So, answer my questions and I'll push no further."

He sighed and shifted to the edge of the bed. Sebastian came undone. He stared at his hands that rested in his lap.

"When Pranske and I were small, we were close. When my home life got unbearable, I'd run over to his place. I've known him since we were young. But what did it matter?" Sebastian snapped, his ego on fire.

"Just tell me."

He huffed out a sigh, clapped his hands together, and continued. "We used to go to chapel, here. We'd sneak into the back row and listen to the goddess stories of unconditional love."

Sebastian spoke carefully, each word censored before it left his mouth.

"Pranske loved the goddess. We both did," Sebastian said, voice dewy with nostalgia. "Do. We both do."

"Did that love turn to hate?"

Sebastian shrugged. "Our friendship sank into a sea of booze."

"You can't keep protecting him. Do you have some unpaid debt to him?" Prentice asked.

"No, I'm not protecting Pranny or anyone!" Sebastian lashed out.

"Could Pranske be vengeful?" Prentice ignored Sebastian's emotional outrage.

Sebastian crossed his arms and shrugged again.

"I'm told he liked getting over on people."

Sebastian squirmed on the bed. "He liked to win. He doesn't backpedal on his threats. When he drank too much ale, he became this angry person. Some people don't like it. By the goddess, this is so wrong. I'm betraying him by telling you this!"

"No, the truth is never the wrong answer," Prentice said.

"You think I like watching the life drain out of him? It tore me apart, and now I'm here, spilling more of his life." Sebastian stood with his hand outstretched.

"The Five-Feathered Crown is missing, Sebastian. You do understand how serious this is. You, Helena, and Pranske were all guards. You had to know the light would fall on you three."

Sebastian glared. "Yes, on us nightjars."

"We're asking Helena the same questions." Prentice started for the door.

"Helena's a nightjar too," Sebastian barked out.

Prentice stopped and turned back to him. "She is."

Sebastian snickered. "For a hawk with your sharp eyes, you miss a lot. She's half nightjar and bluebird."

Prentice nodded, letting the insult roll off her feathers.

"Remember. Someone's going to be held accountable for this."

"Whether we are innocent or not, right, hawk?" Sebastian snatched himself away from her.

"Killion was found dead this morning. Wake up! This is dangerous and the consequences are deadly."

Sebastian gaped and his mouth dropped. "She's dead? How?"

"Someone set her and the museum on fire." Prentice found it odd he hadn't been told. "You didn't know?"

Sebastian blinked. His voice trembled. "No, I...I've been out of it. She stomped on people to get what she wanted, but she didn't deserve this."

He was taken aback, and genuinely upset. Prentice could tell by the way his shoulders and face fell at the news.

"Who would do this to her?" Prentice asked.

He looked at her as if hearing for the first time. His glassy red eyes were like dulled rubies. "She used me, but I loved her anyway."

"Tell me about that."

As he spoke, Prentice noticed cuts on his hand. The wounds looked angry and could've been burns. She couldn't make it out clearly in the dimly lit room.

Sebastian wiped his face. "You already know we courted. But it was far from a warm relationship at the end. I don't know anyone who would kill her."

"What happened to your hand?" Prentice pointed to his left hand.

"Yard work." Sebastian tucked his hand underneath the thin blanket. "Anything else you want to know? I'm tired."

"Just one more thing. Where were you between five and seven this morning?"

"Asleep."

"Can anyone confirm that?" Prentice asked.

"You see anyone here, hawk? You can't see what's so obvious with your special abilities?"

She gleaned what she could from him and ignored his angry words. Grief struck people differently. Sebastian appeared crushed by Killion's death.

Truth wasn't always in appearance.

"I'll leave you to your thoughts."

She left.

By the time she returned to campus, twilight waited in the wings. Lunch had become a distant memory, and Prentice made a beeline for the dining hall. The aromas of delicious grilled fish and chickpeas wafted through the air, snaring passersby and enticing them to come in.

Inside, a hush had descended on the otherwise full seating area. Prentice made a right and went through the line, selecting her food choices. Her nose hadn't deceived her. Grilled trout, caught from the Avian Seas and transported for evening meal, was the highlight. With her trout and salad, she paid the cashier and found the booth at the back available. Once she sat down, she noticed the empty seats she missed when she'd first arrived. Arguably it was early evening, around five, but the back section of the dining area had thinned out.

She forked a piece of fish into her mouth and chewed.

"This is delicious!" she said to herself.

Prentice ate, thinking over the case, but mostly enjoying the time to reflect. She rolled over what she'd learned from Sebastian. His alibi didn't mean he hadn't torched the museum. The drinking vessels could have been old, and the reek that hung in the house attested to a lack of a true cleaning ritual.

"There you are!" Galen shouted from the seating area's archway.

Prentice groaned. Several students looked over to her, and she continued eating, pretending Galen hadn't seen her. Condors didn't do discretion. They lumbered into everything they did.

Galen reached her booth and slid into the opposite seat. "Hoot!"

"Hoot," Prentice said around a bite of lettuce.

"I've been looking for you everywhere. Don't you have your bird caller?"

Prentice paused as she tried to remember where she'd had it last. "I do, but I've been busy interviewing."

"You get anything off the glove?"

"It's Rook Renner's."

Galen sighed. "And the scarf?"

"It belonged to Killion."

Galen raised her hands in defeat.

Prentice swallowed. "It means that whoever killed her didn't plan it. Something happened and the situation escalated. The fire, too, most likely was an afterthought. I'm not ruling anyone out."

Galen crossed her arms. "What else did you find out today? Anything good?"

Prentice shook her head. "Nothing I'm ready to speak on."

"You hawks always play things so close to the breast."

"Well, Sebastian doesn't have anyone to confirm his alibi. Rook Renner claimed Dove Haq can attest to his presence in morning prayers. Zell said her partner can confirm, so can you get one of the eagles to chase that down?"

Galen took out her notepad. "Yes."

"What did you find out today?" Prentice wanted Galen to talk so she could eat the rest of her dinner.

"Helena is being released from medical tomorrow. Pranske is still in a magical coma." Galen read from her notes, her mechanical finger skimming the parchment. "I went back to the coroner for the rest of the autopsy on Killion. She'd been stabbed. The doctor stated the official cause of death is asphyxia via the scarf. The charring was only on the skin, some of her internal organs were unaffected. No reddening in the throat or in the lungs. The way I see it, the assailant gets angry, stabs Killion. She screams. They take the scarf, shove it into her mouth to quiet her. She chokes on it and dies."

Prentice nodded. *A horrible end to such a bright spark. Why would someone want to snuff that out? Jealousy? Revenge?*

"We're missing something here." Prentice wiped her mouth with the cloth napkin.

"Like who stole the Five-Feathered Crown?" Galen quirked an eyebrow.

Prentice peered across to Galen. "Right. That's what started this whole thing. Someone stole the crown. Why? There's been no ransom. No one has tried to sell it. Right?"

"Eagles across Aves are questioning merchants about it.

It's a hot item. No one wants to get their feathers burned handling the crown."

"So, we have a thief who can't unload the item they stole. They don't want money for it, so why steal it in the first place?" Prentice asked.

"Maybe you do get paid by a private collector," Galen offered with a shrug.

"Yes, but you as the private collector could never show it to anyone. One hushed whisper gets loose and that's your life. The Order doesn't take kindly to their goddess items being stolen." Prentice shook her head. "No, the thief didn't steal it for a collector."

Galen smirked. "Okay then. Why was it stolen?"

Prentice forked in salad to give herself time to think. She'd eaten all the fish.

Then it sparked.

"I know that look." Galen sat up straight in her seat.

"The thief used wind magic. That's unique to Edmonds Nest. Before Aves united under the goddess, birds here used it. They created powerful sandstorms and soared above the clouds on rugs. So, who among our list of suspects fits that description?"

Galen flipped pages in her notepad. "Zell is from here, the nightjars, and Helena."

"Killion is an ostrich from Kahassi. Rook Renner is originally from Lanham," Prentice said. "Did you know Helena is half nightjar?"

"No but doesn't mean she has those abilities. Killion and the rook could've conspired with the ones from here to steal the crown."

"Why? Rook Renner wouldn't ruin his reputation. He loves the goddess. I don't see him tarnishing her image."

"Unless he meant to protect it from someone else. So, he hired someone to steal it."

"I don't buy that." Prentice shook her head and lowered her voice. "I need to talk to Helena again."

"She's being released soon. If she goes home, she can disappear into the, well, wind." Galen laughed at her own humor. "Eat up so we can go."

Prentice scowled and climbed out of the booth.

CHAPTER ELEVEN

"She just crept out. Where would she go?" Galen asked.

They stood in the hallway outside Helena's assigned room. The abandoned bed was left in disarray, the blankets scattered, the pillow askew, and the water pitcher turned over. It looked as if someone spooked Helena and she fled. Amazing she'd managed to do so without alarming the geese.

"I came to check on her and get her prepped for release tomorrow," Nurse Aiesha Little said. She stood taller than Prentice, and she held an air of confidence. No doubt, Nurse Little brokered no nonsense on her floor, so Helena's disappearance didn't sit well with her. "That's when I discovered her gone."

"What time was that?" Prentice asked.

"A few hours before you came, hawk." Nurse Little glared at the parchment in her hands. "I notified the doctor on call and the other nurses. We searched but we couldn't find her."

"Did she get any visitors while she was here?" Prentice

took out her notepad and pencil. Something had spooked Helena into running away.

Nurse Little hurried back to the nurses' station, a circle array of desks and parchments, bird callers and quills. Here, the administrative part of healing occurred. She went around to her part of the station and shifted through the scattered items until she found an unrolled scroll.

"Ah, yes, here is a list of visitors for Helena." She handed it to Prentice. "We were in the process of discharging her."

Prentice and Galen took the scroll over to the hallway, away from the nurses' station so they wouldn't be overheard.

Helena sure was a popular bird.

Prentice read the names aloud for Galen to hear. "Me. Paige, the dove's secretary, Sebastian, Rook Renner, and the last person to see her was Zell."

"Zell? I thought she hated everyone." Galen scowled.

"I believe that's a front, a mask. I suspect Zell has many more ties than she'd like to reveal to her colleagues. Note the time, Galen."

Prentice lifted the scroll up and over so Galen could read the script beside Zell's name.

"That's two hours ago."

"After Zell's visit, Helena left." Prentice rolled the scroll up and handed it to Galen. "Keep this in your satchel. We'll need it later."

Galen did as instructed. "Now what?"

"I think I know where Helena went. Come on. We'll need a carriage." Prentice headed toward the exit. "Thank you, Nurse Little. You've been a big help."

Nurse Little waved a goodbye and returned to her duties.

Galen took out her bird caller. "To where? I need to tell the driver."

"We're headed to Sebastian's house out in Sulidae, on its east side, to the Nightendale neighborhood."

"You think she went to Sebastian's?"

"Yes, I think this whole thing ties back to the nightjars, just as you suspected."

Galen's eyebrows rose. Her milky eye closed as she winked at Prentice. "That'd be a first."

They reached the bottom floor when Prentice said, "But not for the reason you think."

"Awww."

"There's a feeling in my feathers that I've missed something big, something I should've seen earlier."

"What?" Galen asked.

"Let me sit with it a little while longer, Galen. I promise I'll explain. I just need to check a few more things," Prentice sighed.

"Such as?"

"Zell's alibi. I haven't circled back to talk to the partner. She wasn't home when I interviewed Zell earlier."

Galen nodded. "I got an eagle following up on it, but I can go over there. We can split up."

Prentice shook her head. "I need you with me on this. It could get heated, and if Helena is there, like I suspect, covering her and Sebastian might be more than I can handle."

"They wouldn't attack you." Galen scoffed.

"Someone killed Killion and burned down the museum. They also cut off Pranske's hands with wind magic."

"Right," Galen said. "Great. There's the carriage."

They walked from the medical building to the university's front entrance. A clear evening presented beauty and tranquility. A hush had fallen over the campus and the usual shouting, noise, excitement, and zeal of student interaction had been muted. It was as if everyone mourned the loss of both Killion and the museum. The bubble had burst, and students walked around stunned.

Prentice longed to ease the burden and suspicion that had befallen the campus community. She had to get this solved and soon so things could go back to normal. And so that those impacted could heal.

The eagle driver greeted them. "Hoot, Condor Gar. Hawk Tasifa. My supervisor said you need a ride out to Nightendale?"

"Yes," Prentice opened the carriage door and hoisted herself inside, skipping the need for the steps.

"Sir, Nightendale is quite dangerous in the evenings. The nightjars are active now, and it can be, well, violent." The eagle looked uncomfortable in his one-piece green uniform and black combat boots. He carried a baton at this side. It matched his boots. And his assumptions.

Galen looked up at him. "No more dangerous than any other neighborhood. What's the address, Pren?"

Prentice gave them the address.

Galen climbed into the carriage and slammed the door. She locked it from the inside and knocked on the panel behind Prentice. "Let's go!"

The carriage lunged forward as the horses set off in a trot.

Prentice sat back and crossed her legs. Galen sat across from her.

Galen smirked. "I know that look. You know what happened."

"I have a theory."

"Spill it."

"Galen…"

"Oh, come on! If you get it wrong, no one's going to take your talons."

"I'm still working it out. This is why I prefer to work alone." Prentice uncrossed her legs and leaned forward.

Galen laughed. "You love me."

Prentice paused, and then said, "Rook Renner asked me why the crown was stolen now. It's been on display in the museum since its discovery. He'd been the curator for the Museum of the Goddess for decades. So why now?"

"And?"

"When I talked to him today, he mentioned how it seemed that someone targeted him. The ledger in his office directly denounces the rumor that he stole birdsong from the museum. The account was in the black. Sure, the glove that I found was his, but it was his office."

"So, what you're saying is someone is doing a bang-up job trying to ruin Rook Renner."

"It would appear. The crown's theft puts him in a negative light. The stealing of money from the museum, and the death of one of his employees, not including the inappropriate relationship between Sebastian and Killion all painted him as unfit in his duties." Prentice used her fingers for a display. "One. Rook Renner didn't steal the crown. He has an airtight alibi, which you would assume the thief would've known. Two. He readily turned over all the monthly ledgers to the court's bookkeepers. Nothing has come of those yet or he'd be in a birdcage. Three.

Killion's and Sebastian's relationship gets aired and the rook gets questioned from the dove about why he allowed it to continue. Now, normally, it wouldn't be a huge to do but in light of the other shenanigans at the museum it looks more and more like Rook Renner can't handle the job."

Galen's mouth made a round o. "Who would want his job?"

"Two people wanted it: Zell and Killion, who, until today, I thought were rivals. Zell's reaction to Killion's death changed that."

"Howdid she react?"

Prentice filled Galen in on the interview with Zell earlier that morning.

"That's strange. So, they were *close* friends. I mean, she had a nickname for her and everything."

"Indeed." Prentice sat back and closed her eyes. "You should relax until we get there."

"What are you expecting to happen, Pren?"

"I just have a feeling in my feathers. That's all."

"Well, that's enough for me."

Prentice gazed out of the carriage window to the familiar landscape she spied earlier in the afternoon. As the day sank into evening, the feel of the streets and the atmosphere shifted to one of excitement and thrill. Lanterns lit along the sidewalks and festive eateries transitioned from lunch to dinner. The fragrance of wine and ale now scented the air, and the sweet smell of roasted corn and fish slipped through the carriage's closed windows. She had eaten dinner, but she didn't know how Galen continued to not eat or drink.

Perhaps she did, just not with Prentice. Condors ate

carrion, like vultures, and the dead, fleshy meat and its hideous odor appealed to them in ways it didn't for other birds. A separation in restaurants and other places emerged. It was difficult to find places that provided birdfeed and carrion on the menu. Condors could also go for long periods without food or drink. Either way, it concerned her. She wanted Galen at her full strength.

Helena was shaken up. Messy hair and bruises on her forearms where she had been restrained in the medical bed added to her dishevelment. She huddled close to Sebastian, who was jittery.

"I didn't like her. Just because she's dead doesn't mean I'm gonna say nice things," Helena's face pinched in a frown.

Galen cleared her throat. "No, but we know you know something about her death."

Helena could be easily led. So could Sebastian. There had to be a leader. Who had enough charisma to make people give up themselves for something bigger?

"I know you were involved. Tell me everything." Prentice gestured to them. "Start at the beginning, wherever you think that is."

"You don't know anything," Sebastian said. He wrapped his arm around Helena's shoulders.

"Explain your whereabouts," Prentice said, ignoring Sebastian.

Helena was the key that just needed to be turned. She avoided eye contact.

"I told you. I was here," Sebastian said.

"Helena, he can't prove he was here," Prentice said.

"You can't prove I wasn't here," Sebastian said.

"I know you're all friends, but friendship has its limits. Slaying is that line." Prentice stood. "This senseless destruction is at an end. This wasn't some awful accident."

"Talk. A sharp knife cuts clean." Galen removed her sword.

Helena's eyes showed too much white. She broke Sebastian's hold and slid down the wall to the floor. Tears left salt trails down her cheeks.

"I had no idea things would unfold this way," she said. She wiped her face. "We're members of the Goddess is Greater chapel, here in Nightendale."

"That's a fringe group. They don't follow all of the teachings." Galen started.

Prentice held up her hand to silence her. Now that Helena began to talk, Prentice wanted to hear it all.

Sebastian blew out a huff. "The three of us are members. We worship a purer approach and interpretation of the goddess's teachings. A few of the members practice wind magic." He sounded authentic and more than a little afraid.

"Three being you two plus Pranske," Prentice said.

"Yes," Helena whispered. Prentice saw the blood pumping. It made the vein in her throat jump. "I was afraid to disappoint him."

"Him?"

"Prankse." Helena chewed on her bottom lip.

"How did Killion come to be a member?" Prentice asked. "You Sebastian?"

"Yeah. She wanted to know more about our beliefs, so she could feed it to her students like bloated, fat worms.

She attended a few sessions." He put his head in his hands. "Pranske was furious. Something about her ignited his temper. He wanted her to stop going. He said she polluted things."

"But she didn't stop going. Did she?" Prentice pushed a little more. She had to get all of it, the blackened glob of deceit and betrayal they'd dropped all over the campus. "Did she!"

"No! Okay? No. She fell under the dove's sway." Sebastian ran a punishing hand through his hair.

"The dove? You sully the position of The Order within that dung smear of a sect?" Galen barked.

Prentice shot her look to shut up.

Helena's head snapped up at Galen's outburst. "No! We wouldn't dare take on The Order's disgusting practices. The leader of the GIG is called the Ocho."

Prentice didn't care about that. She had much bigger worms to get. "Was Killion killed for her trouble?"

Sebastian wiped his tears with the back of his hand. "I dunno why she was killed or whodunnit."

Prentice saw into him. A lonely and bleak existence, living in a wreck of a house. His hopes and dreams were to get away, but that hadn't happened. Sebastian pushed himself to a standing position.

"Killion used you, Sebastian. She used *all* of you. She launched a smear campaign against Rook Renner. She started the embezzlement rumor. When it didn't get the rook dismissed from his position, she came up with the heist." Prentice waited to see what impact her words had.

Helena nodded.

Sebastian cried. "They made me sick. I wanted to get out of this hellhole, but no. Once Killion went to the first meeting, she became like a bird on fire, a phoenix like the goddess herself, determined to rise from her own ashes. She and Pranske were in attendance every time the chapel doors opened."

Helena hugged him close. "See. He couldn't have killed Killion. Look how heartbroken he is about all this."

"People are capable of horrific acts when they're emotional. The more emotional, the more horrific and violent, in my experience," Prentice said. Still, her heart pinched for Sebastian. All he ever wanted was a life and that was taken from him. She wasn't about to share that with Helena or anyone. Her empathy notwithstanding, he could've slayed Killion and burned down the museum.

"That's why you switched shifts. Killion didn't want you there. She probably knew you'd fail to support her with Pranske. Helena is a true believer."

Helena didn't deny it.

"I need a minute to myself," Sebastian stalked out the front door, leaving it ajar.

Galen followed him outside.

Sebastian was afraid and fear made people dangerous.

"Helena, Killion stole the Five-Feathered crown. Didn't she?" Prentice asked as the puzzle piece clicked into place.

The longer she spoke to them, the more comfortable Helena became. She stared out the opened front door. "Pranske would launch into jealous rages. He despised Killion and her relationship with Sebastian."

"What happened, Helena?" Prentice turned her attention to the crumpled woman on the floor.

Helena cleared her throat. "That night Killion hid in Rook Renner's office. He had late lecture, and Pranny didn't sweep that area. We locked up. Did the usual closing routine. The thief dropped out of her hiding place. Before I could stop him, Pranny attacked her. She hadn't expected him, but then she used her wind magic to hurt Pranny and me."

Her flat, emotionless voice ended.

"Why such savagery for Pranske?" Prentice asked. That detail bothered her. A head injury for Helena, but Pranske's hands were cut off. Killion didn't seem capable of it, but appearances could deceive. It didn't *feel* right.

"Where's the crown?" Galen asked from the doorway. Sebastian stood in front of her.

"I dunno. Ask him!" Helena pointed at Sebastian.

"She didn't tell me," Sebastian said. "She wouldn't speak to me outside of work and museum matters afterwards."

"Did you know it was Killion who stole the crown?" Prentice asked.

"No. I didn't know anything about what they'd cooked up." He cast his eyes downward, staring at his sandaled feet.

"Did either of you kill Killion?" Prentice shifted the conversation.

"No," they said in unison.

"Galen, I want searches on everyone's residences."

"What?" Helena came up from the floor, arms flailing as if trying to grip air to stand.

Galen ran, jumped, and took flight, soaring back to the university campus.

Prentice turned back to Helena and Sebastian. "That crown is somewhere. Close. In Sulidae. I know you know more, Helena."

"You don't know anything," Helena said.

Sebastian stood stone-faced.

"That's the second time I've heard that from you two. I'll be back. Don't fly off." Prentice ordered and left. She could've pushed Helena a little more, but she wanted the young bird to think she'd won.

Once outside, Prentice hurried to the waiting carriage and headed back to the university. Alone, she replayed the new information. Sebastian said plainly he wasn't privy to what they cooked up. As the formation began to take shape, she shook her feathers in anticipation. Helena and who? Killion? The two of them together planned the crown heist. It would explain why Helena had only a head injury and some debris damage to her arms, while Pranske was mutilated.

Her attention returned to Pranske. Why cut off his hands? Prentice couldn't shake the feeling that the answers revolved around the use of wind magic and the lashing out at him, specifically. Why such a severe injury to him? It seemed personal. Sure, Killion didn't like Pranske or vice versa. According to Zell, the relationship with Sebastian didn't mean that much to Killion, but Pranske thought it did. Zell also said Pranske had threatened Killion. Did that warrant her slicing off his hands?

No.

Prentice wasn't sold on the ostrich spinning wind magic either. Ostriches didn't fly or possess the magic to do so. Most of them, if they had any magic abilities were earth mages, but it even that was rare. Prentice closed her eyes.

Could Sebastian have done it?

How? He wasn't there that evening, but she only had his and Helena's word. If only Pranske would wake up. She could get to the bottom of this. He could confirm or invalidate Helena's statement and provide more eyewitness testimony.

Zell might be behind the theft, but it didn't seem likely. She acted on Killion's word when she reported Rook Renner's alleged embezzlement. She and Killion had been friends—not that it meant she wouldn't slay the ostrich. Prentice couldn't find a motive. She needed to confirm the alibi, but otherwise, Zell moved down the list of suspects.

Sebastian, despite his temper flaring, was still a follower. Helena's terse yes and no answers hinted at deception.

I need additional information!

Prentice couldn't shake that she'd missed something. It wiggled like an itch she couldn't scratch.

CHAPTER TWELVE

Once Prentice arrived back at campus, she went to her apartment and removed her belts, leaving her talons on the table. With frustration making her angry, she climbed onto the full-sized bed. She had an idea. She couldn't get Pranske's point of view of what happened, but she had her own; when she reviewed the scene with her hawk eyes a day before the fire. The museum fire destroyed the residual essence. All that remained was in her memory. She couldn't use her hawk abilities, but she had other skills. The blade she kept on her belt, now rested beside her thigh.

She sat cross-legged on the bed before extending her wings. They beat slow and steady, increasing until she hovered several inches above the bed. Once she unsheathed the knife, she extended her index finger and drew the sharp blade across the finger pad.

Prentice hissed, but she spread it across her other nine fingers. Next, she clasped both palms together and rotated her hands in the opposite directions, like the eyespots of a peacock, fingers splayed. She closed her eyes, feeling the wound throb.

As she focused, she used the high speech. *"Voir avec les yeux d'un paon."*

Her fingers became the peacock's purple eyespots before becoming human again and opened. They poured a wave of cerulean blue light into the room, the magic crashing into Prentice, illuminating the back of her eyelids. Each of the eyespots reflected a different recent memory. She sighed as her body broke out in a sweat. The Eyes of the Peacock ritual required a chunk of magic. The enchantment slammed into her and she fell spiritually into the first opened eyespot, the iris rippling as she disturbed the surface. The memory returned her to the museum.

As she walked within the space, she took in more of the setting, seeing the magnificent museum and its glass-covered displays and immaculate treasures with appreciative eyes. She'd engaged her hawk eyes and the vision she witnessed replayed in vivid color. The memory was so sharp Prentice wanted to reach out and touch items now destroyed by fire.

Motion snared her attention. Prentice watched as Killion, cloaked and hooded, emerged from Rook Renner's office. Her navy-toned neck flashed briefly in the lights. She scurried to the guarded section where the crown and other high-value items were on display. Prentice hadn't caught that detail when she searched the museum the first time. She hadn't spied the ostrich's neck, but she followed Killion as she hurried to the main display room.

The world swept left to Pranske and Helena doing their closing activities. Prentice had to orient herself. Once they secured and locked the front door, they returned to their posts. Prentice sighed. She *knew* she'd missed something but thus far it followed Helena's statement. The confrontation, the wind magic, and the scene ended with the thief, Killion, racing from the museum, using the front entrance and unlocking it with ease.

"*Repeate,*" Prentice said aloud. Her limbs trembled from the strain. Her wings shuddered in warning. The Peacock Eyes took chunks of magic to keep the portals open. She winced when she dropped to the bed with a *thud*.

The memory commenced again as Prentice bent over in pain.

By the sixth review, Prentice saw it.

As Killion jumped down from the beams, Helena spied her. Pranske did, too, a moment after her. Killion raised her hand, shouted an incantation, and it sent Helena flying into the wall. Just as Prentice's hawk eyes spied five times before.

But now, something caught her eye.

"There!" Prentice said aloud.

In the resurrected scene, Helena made a hand gesture, small, by her right leg, as she muttered something.

At first, Prentice assumed Helena was yelling at the thief to stop. So focused on the thief, Prentice hadn't paid much attention to the guards. After multiple reviews, Prentice saw Pranske's order to stop, didn't match Helena's lip movement. She wasn't saying stop. What was Helena saying?

The attack on Pranske happened a moment after Prentice saw Helena, not unconscious, but injured, make the same hand gesture, and mouthed more muted words.

And again, as Killion stole the crown, lifting the glass with wind magic.

Killion wasn't using wind magic.

Helena was.

"Helena's the wind user."

Prentice vaulted up in the bed, legs trembling as she scrambled out of its comfort. She snatched on her belts, her hands blood-stained and shaking. Her dress was plastered to her back and sticking to her legs. Prentice's mind raced over all the things she heard from Helena. She reviewed every conversation and admonished herself for missing the now obvious clues.

It was a kick in the gut.

Before leaving, Prentice took out her bird caller. With effort, she blew into it.

It squawked until Galen answered. "Yeah?"

"It's Helena. She's the wind user," Prentice said, locking her door behind her.

Galen said, "I'll be there. Where are you?"

"I'm leaving my rental. Look, get eagles on it. We need to find Helena now."

"Stay there. I'm on my way."

Prentice stopped outside in the evening twilight. "Galen, tell them to be careful and don't approach her. She can use wind to suck out their guts."

Prentice couldn't just wait for the eagles to find Helena. The campus settled down for the evening. Summer breezes blew through the palms and rustled Prentice's headwrap. Her limbs shook with fatigue. She took off at a slow run and leapt into the air, attempting to launch. Her wings flapped, but she couldn't get enough lift. The ground came fast and hard. Prentice lay there crumpled against the pavement and struggled to push herself to an upright position. Her pride hurt more than her limbs.

Several students giggled and laughed, but a couple shouted out in concern.

Prentice ignored all of them. The Eyes of the Peacock ritual took an entire 24 hours to recover. A healing spell wouldn't help because she didn't suffer a physical injury.

After a few minutes, she got up. Every part of her body dangled like a puppet with its strings cut. As she made her way back to the apartment, the pieces of Helena's betrayal solidified in her mind. Prentice's body may have been ragged, but her mind remained sharp.

What happened to Pranske was an emotional attack. How long had Helena spent stewing in jealousy of his relationship with Sebastian and more, Sebastian's forgiving nature? She lashed out in fury at Pranske. With his history of intimidating people, Pranske suffered.

Weakened, Prentice let herself in the room and collapsed onto the bed.

Minutes later, Galen arrived, pushing through the unlocked door. She slammed it shut and secured it. When she spied Prentice on the bed, she hurried over to her.

"What the hell?"

"I rattled her," Prentice said.

"Who?" Galen frowned. "What?"

"Helena."

Galen's mouth twitched. "Helena? Our meek little guard?"

"The guard. Yes. Meek? No. She's the mastermind and orchestrator of a conspiracy." Prentice cursed herself as she tried to push herself up on her elbows. "She had first-hand knowledge of the theft. She just didn't tell it to us."

I should've seen it sooner.

Prentice hadn't gotten the chance to interview Pranske.

"Helena made sure Pranske suffered enough to kill him, but to her surprise he didn't die. The ravens kept him unconscious, but she still had to change her plan."

"Wait a minute. Slow down Pren…"

"Think on it, Galen. We only have Helena's eyewitness account. No clues. The bicycle belonged to Sebastian, but it can't be confirmed. The bicycle prints could've been there for days, maybe even weeks. Helena meant to kill him, but the injury she gave herself was more serious than she intended."

"Kill Sebastian?"

"No. Pranske!" Prentice fell backward onto the bed.

"Pren, slow down. What have you done to yourself?" Galen set about removing Prentice's shoes. She took Prentice's ankles and dragged them fully onto the bed.

"There's no time. That's what I'm trying to tell you." Prentice shook her head and tried again to get up.

"Killion stole the crown," Galen offered.

"Yes. Manipulated by Helena, though I doubt she knew," Prentice said. "Killion was never a wind user. Helena was. She convinced the ostrich that she could use those abilities, when in fact, it was Helena invoking the magic. That's why Sebastian had to switch shifts with her."

"Lie back down and for the love of the goddess, rest!"

"Pranske and Sebastian were like brothers. She completed their trio. The ocho, the head of that goddess cult is probably Helena. She discovered her wind magic and that made her a *goddess* to them."

Galen shook her head. "She seemed so sweet."

"Like hummingbird water."

Galen groaned. "So, she was in love with Pranske."

"No. Sebastian. Over time, Helena watched Pranske

abuse Sebastian. By all accounts, he used vindictive tactics."

Galen folded her arm across her chest. "He bullied Killion, who we now know was Helena's disciple."

"Whatever relationship they had must have soured."

Galen sighed. "You need to rest."

"Once the rage subsided, Helena had to figure out how to get away." Prentice shook her head. "I want to put this harrowing ordeal to an end."

"Let's find the crown." Galen set a bottle of sweet milk on the table. "This should help. You sounded weak as a chick's first flight on the caller."

"Thank you!" Prentice grabbed the bottle just as Galen removed the cork. "You've been talking almost non-stop. Which ritual did you perform?"

"The Eyes of Peacock."

Galen stiffened. "Prentice, that's almost mage level blood magic."

Prentice gulped down the sweet milk, using it as a perfect reason not to respond. The idea felt right. Helena had ascended to cult level leader or as a dove to her followers. She'd use the crown as a touchstone for them, confirmation of her power.

Galen waited. "Tell me."

"The crown hasn't left this egg." Prentice sucked in a steadying breath and stood. Her legs buckled almost at once, sending the milk sloshing inside the bottle. "We need to go back to Nightendale. We'll probably find Helena there and the crown."

Galen shrugged. "We searched each of the suspects' residences. They didn't find anything. Besides, you aren't fit to go anywhere right now."

"Oh, it isn't at a residence. It's in a chapel." Prentice rubbed her face and stood up again. This time she stepped toward the door on stronger, albeit still weak, legs. "I got a feeling in my feathers."

"You should wait. I don't see the reason to rush, Pren."

"The carriage waiting?"

Galen laughed. "Yeah."

"Let's soar."

She followed Galen out. The sweet milk helped restore some of her energy. Still weakened, Prentice took small steps, but it would have to do. They exited the faculty apartments to a waiting carriage at the main entrance.

The eagle driver drove like an enraged rooster to get them to Nightendale.

"You asked me about the rush."

Galen nodded.

"Helena knows we are searching their homes, she will move the crown. If we wait, it might be carted outside the egg and then it's gone forever," Prentice explained.

Galen leaned forward in her seat. "How did you know? You're sure about this."

"The Peacock eyes showed me. I was able to see the unseen bits I missed."

The tendrils of night stretched throughout the Sulidae egg by the time Prentice and Galen arrived in Nightendale. As she expected, the neighborhood burst with light and activity, a thousand fireflies set loose in the summer sky. Unlike the deadened and hushed afternoon quiet, dozens of nightjars stood around in groups, huddled together every so many feet. Music clashed as it floated out of opened doors. The many aromas melded into a mixture of spicy deliciousness so strong, Prentice wished she could bite the air. As their carriage made its way to Sebastian's, the conversations amongst those outside and close to the road stopped. Nightjars watched them with vibrant scarlet eyes.

"Stick out like a pigeon feather," Galen said, but she kept her gaze cast on the outside.

"Mmhm." Prentice studied the buildings clustered together.

The chapel couldn't be far from the homes. Often, like the chapel on campus and in Gould, the place of goddess gathering resided at the heart of the neighborhood. The nightjars' devotion to the goddess ensured they'd follow along with the same tradition. The Order didn't embrace their teachings or beliefs about the goddess, but instead of outright denouncing them, they kept a wary eye on them.

"What are you looking for?" Galen asked.

"The chapel. The one in which Helena acts as a dove. It has to be close."

Soon, they reached Sebastian's residence, and the carriage rolled to a stop. Prentice got out first. The velvety night sparkled with stars, but one burned brighter than the others.

"There!" She pointed to Galen, who stuck her head out of the door. "There's the chapel."

Galen peered. "How far away is that? You can only see the goddess's flames from here."

"It's in the center of the houses. Let's get Sebastian. I bet he knows the way." Prentice started for his front door.

Once she reached it, she found it ajar. She took out both

talons and slowed her approach. Her hands ached and her fingers struggled to remain wrapped around her weapons. Inside the entranceway, shadows huddled together. Prentice stopped two feet from the door.

"Sebastian! Come out." She raised her talons and pointed them at the opened gap. Whispers snaked out to greet her. "Sebastian!"

Galen approached on her left, her sword unsheathed and in hand, her muscles clenched.

Prentice didn't want to blow through the first person who walked out. So, she waited, placing one of the talons away.

"One more moment, Sebastian. Then I'm coming in," Prentice called. "I just want to talk."

At this, Sebastian stumbled out of the house. The door shut behind him.

His glittering red eyes spied the weapons, and he raised his arms in the air. "You said talk, hawk."

Prentice lowered her other talon and reholstered it. "I need you to take us to chapel."

Sebastian lowered his arms. "Why? Service is over."

Galen didn't lower her sword. "Take. Us. Now."

"Okay. Okay." Sebastian adjusted his pants, yanking them up to his waist. "Follow me."

He didn't bother telling his houseguests that he was leaving. With his shoulders hunched against the dark, he snatched up the lantern from the porch and led the way down the dirt-packed path around his house, heading east, before making a left. This led them through the homes behind Sebastian's and deeper into the Nightendale neighborhood. The scent of yucca and palm trees fragranced the cooler evening air. Crickets called to their lovers, but the trio remained quiet. Prentice glanced to her left and spied Galen. She had sheathed the sword, but kept her hand wrapped around the hilt. Ahead, Sebastian led without turning to see if they followed. Every few feet lanterns cast glowing arcs of light, illuminating the way toward the chapel.

Prentice's limbs felt heavy. Each step took effort and she longed to lay down right there along the path and sleep. She gritted her teeth and pushed on.

Galen was right. I should've rested. But she knew she couldn't because her hunch demanded she resolve the missing crown issue.

They made turns and got closer, the air sweetened with the scent of jasmine and lavender, the goddess's odors. The dirt path soon blended into smooth terracotta squares that broadened all the way to the building's wooden front doors.

Conversations sprung up to greet them as they turned the corner. Prentice spied loose clusters of birds, talking and squawking amongst each other. Service had ended, but the post service conversations lingered. People enjoyed themselves, laughing and talking.

"Looks like service has just ended," Prentice said to Galen, keeping her voice low.

"It's the service after the service," Galen remarked. "Birds like to flock together."

Acoustic guitar music poured out of the open doors. It served as accompaniment to the guffaws and chatter. The relaxed atmosphere held an undercurrent of tension, small, but it was there. Shuffling of feet, the increased speed of conversations, the tightness around the smiles and the red eyes all pointed to an uncomfortableness.

When one of the members spied Sebastian, he raised his hand in greeting. "Sebastian! I thought you'd headed home for the usual game of cards."

Before Sebastian could answer, the bird spied Prentice, and he lowered his hand and closed his mouth. He turned away from Sebastian and whispered to someone in their group. Prentice couldn't see because Sebastian blocked her view, but she put her hand on one of her talons anyway. Muffled voices rose around them.

As they reached the chapel's plaza, the buzzing conversations ceased. All glittering red eyes were on them. The music continued to stream out from the chapel and the air thickened with lavender.

"What do you want?" a man demanded as he stepped into the pathway, blocking their path. He gestured to Sebastian to step aside. He wore a long, ivory thobe and a decorative bishet that had the goddess's flames embroidered on it, sandals, and a ghutra with a black egal. "This is a private ceremony."

"Hoot. I'm Hawk Tasifa." Prentice extended her hand in greeting. "I'm here on a behalf of The Order."

"The Order?" the man balked and refused to shake her hand.

"Who are you?" Prentice dropped her hand but held his gaze.

"It doesn't matter who I am. You can't enter here." He hitched up his chin.

Galen closed the distance between herself and the man. "You aren't the dove for this chapel. It falls under the scope of Dove Raz Haq. So, either show us your wings or get out of the way."

"In case you're lost, this is Nightendale. We do not answer to the Raz Haq." He swallowed hard.

Prentice waved Galen back. "But you aren't the dove. Are you?"

"No..." he puffed out.

"Then, you can't speak for this chapel. Move out of the way," Prentice said. She gestured to Sebastian to go ahead.

Loud chattering erupted around them.

Slayings always draw a crowd.

Sebastian headed inside the chapel. Another bird sought to stop him, but he shook her off with a scowl. Prentice had a feeling that Sebastian had seen enough and wanted the entire ordeal to be over. Perhaps he did love Killion and her death had made everything real and raw for him.

After a few minutes of tense standoff, the music inside stopped. Then a woman appeared at the door's entrance.

"Hoot." Prentice offered in greeting.

"What do you want?" The speaker was a tall woman; a crow with a long beak like nose and dark, piercing eyes. Her dark hair had been braided into a solitary plait. Sharp cheekbones that could cut glass became an attractive visage.

"I'm sure Sebastian told you." Prentice nodded at Sebastian who stood in the background.

"Come inside, Hawk Tasifa." The woman waved her forward.

"Galen?" Prentice met her eye.

"Got it covered out here." She nodded.

"Don't kill anyone."

"No promises, sir." Galen laughed. "I know what's at stake."

It was a cold, mirthless cackle.

Prentice saw some of the members start to wonder off the plaza, leaving to home or other gatherings. She followed the woman inside the chapel.

"What do you want here?" The woman hitched her chin high. "Why are you here?"

"I'm Hawk Tasifa," Prentice repeated. "And you are?"

"I am Siete in the high speech." Siete stiffened.

"Seven."

She nodded.

"Is Helena here?"

"The Ocho? No, she isn't here," Siete said.

"Eight?"

"Oh, yes. To us, Ocho is holy. It is infinity. It is a continued connectedness of all," Siete said with fervor.

"The infinity symbol isn't an eight," Prentice said.

"It is all about your perspective, hawk," Siete replied coolly.

"Does every member get a number?" Prentice asked.

Siete glared. "No. Only those who have a special connectedness with the goddess."

"Wind magic?"

"It is forbidden for me to say more. The goddess selects those she deems worthy." Siete crossed her arms.

Sure. It's forbidden. That's why you can't say.

Prentice forced her face to remain blank. "I'm investigating the theft of the Five Feathered Crown, the museum arson, and slaying of a faculty member that occurred on campus."

"I see." Siete's face tightened.

"I need to search this chapel."

Siete licked her thin lips. "We have nothing to hide here. Come."

"You haven't seen the Five Feathered Crown here?" Prentice asked, as she walked from the foyer into the inner sections.

Inside, a wall to wall mosaic floor tile with a giant gold eight in its center greeted them. Beside Prentice, Siete walked, her beige gown flowing in a hush across the flooring. She swept her hand out across the beautiful space.

"See? There is no crown here."

Prentice ignored her. It had to be here, and Siete had most likely seen it. All of the members, no doubt had. Their secretive manner, their hushed conversation and quick retreat when she arrived all spoke to their duplicity in its theft. Siete didn't feel shame or guilt, but she did want Prentice to leave. Her body language basically screamed it.

"I know it's here, Siete. I know Helena showed you all the sacrifice that Killion gave for the goddess."

All of the color drained out of her face.

Prentice waited.

The lying was part of them getting what they want.

Siete walked away, circling the floral arrangement as if she couldn't stand still.

"The façade Helena showed you isn't the person that she truly is," Prentice said.

Siete hissed. "Silence! You dare? You stand in the holy place, overseen by The Ocho, and you speak ill of her?"

Prentice stretched her wings. "I'm a hawk, Siete. I see the unseen. All of Aves is searching for that crown. You're in enough trouble with The Order as it is. If I tell them you cooperated with my investigation, they may not give you death. Helena has fled. Leaving the crown with you and leaving you to have your wings clipped."

"I don't want to be involved in this." Siete snatched herself away. She stalked off down the corridor, leaving Prentice standing alone in the prayer room.

Prentice decided not to follow. Instead, she began checking the pillars inside the chapel space. She knocked on them, looking for one that may be hollow to hold a treasure like the crown. The process took time. The more she searched, the more energy she expelled and at this point, she didn't have much left.

Siete would either believe her or not. People like others who tell them how special they are. No doubt, Helena told all of her disciples they belonged here; Wind users were given numbers to separate them from the others and elevate them.

Finding nothing there, Prentice made her way to narrowing sections reserved for the dove, or rather here, The Ocho. It wasn't a sacred place. Prentice went into the carpeted area. Here, thick mauve pillows provided places to sit. She felt around the beneath the pillows and along the raised dais.

Nothing.

Prentice put her hands on her hips. Sweat dripped from her and she wiped her face with the back of her hand. Her feathers ruffled. She tossed her head back in frustration and searched the exposed beams and the roof's thatch work.

The glittering caught her eye.

"No one ever looks up," Prentice muttered to herself.

She flapped her wings, and then jumped, sending her into the air. Prentice flew up to the rafters and found The

Five Feathered Crown sitting at the intersection of the beams. It hadn't been placed in a bag or anything to protect it. If it had fallen, it would have shattered.

"Careless." Prentice flew down to the ground, the crown in her fist, and she collapsed to the floor. The cool tile felt good against her burning skin.

Siete was nowhere to be found, probably alerting Helena about the crown.

"I've got to get out of here," Prentice whispered. The irony of hiding a stolen item in a holy place was lost on them.

She closed her eyes and waited for enough strength to leave. When she opened her eyes, the candles had been snuffed out and the room lay in shadows.

Prentice exited the chapel, closing the doors after her. The groups had dispersed, and she found Galen seated on the raised wall filled with yucca and various succulents.

"Took you long enough. Did you search the toilets too?" Galen asked.

"You could've come to check on me." Prentice walked over to Galen who nibbled on a bit of carrion.

"Get what you want?" She threw the bone off into the yard.

"Yes." Prentice held up the crown.

"Nice!" Galen reached out to touch it.

"We need to talk to Dove Haq first thing in the morning and return this," Prentice said. She removed her head wrap and wrapped the crown in it. No need to get mugged. "Where's Sebastian?"

Galen wiped her mouth on her sleeve. "I sent him home. He isn't going anywhere."

"Any luck finding Helena?" Prentice started back the way they'd come.

"No," Galen said. "The eagles searched her home, and talked to her extended family, but no one has seen her."

The overhead sky had grown darker and now shone with lights, but they dimmed. The crown seemed heavy in the crook of her arm, but Prentice was relieved to have found it. She still had no idea who set the museum fire that killed Killion. Why would Helena slay her favorite disciple?

Once they reached the carriage, they found the eagle driver with his head tucked into his bosom, sound asleep. The nightjars had moved their party away from Sebastian's house and into other parts of the neighborhood. Laughs, music, and the aroma of grilled food whirled on the wind.

"Someone's having a good time." Galen remarked as she shook the horses' reigns. The driver spooked awake.

"Sorry ma'am." He cleared his throat and shuddered awake.

"Take us back to university," Galen said, smirking at the eagle.

She and Prentice climbed into the carriage. Fatigue would wait no longer. Her body relaxed against the seat, and she closed her eyes. Sleep pushed through her desire to remain awake.

As they headed back to campus, Prentice wondered about Helena's whereabouts.

She was out there, in the dark, looking for another victim or a chance to escape.

CHAPTER THIRTEEN

Paige Christie, the dove's secretary, peered over her rolls of parchment and desk cactus at Prentice and Galen. She held a quill in on hand, and curiosity in the other. Prentice adjusted her pillow and glanced across to Galen. They arrived after lunch with the crown folded in Prentice's headwrap from last night. She had another scarf holding her hair tied up today, this one with bright purple streaks in a sea of black. She wore her matching ebony dress and sandals, but she wished she hadn't eaten the garlic in her salad.

"You look like you swallowed a spoon," Galen whispered across to her. She had her arms crossed, the mechanical fingers drumming on the other forearm.

"I'm fine."

"No, you're not. You need at least twelve more hours of sleep."

"Not going to happen. I'm fine," Prentice said.

She looked across to Paige again. They'd been waiting for close to an hour to meet with Dove Haq. Not telling

Paige they had the crown may have been an error. The crown bit into the bend in her arm. It felt heavy against her lap, and she wanted it gone. Then she could discover the meatier parts of this investigation that haven't been resolved; loose ends that deserved to be tied off.

Prentice also had a feeling the dove made them wait on purpose as punishment for not checking in more often and submitting to the strict protocol most Order investigations required.

The hottest part of the day had come and gone. Small breezes rustled parchment and scrolls before leaving via the windows again. Candles flickered and the scents of grilled fish settled inside the room.

At once, the door to Dove Haq's office swung open. She swept out in a gown billowing with soft ivory sleeves, flowing fabric down to her feet, and a short matching train at her back. She waved at Prentice in her usual cold demeanor.

"Come. Bring the other one, too," Dove Haq said, and without waiting, turned and went back into her office.

Prentice and Galen got up from their pillows and followed.

Once inside the office, Dove Haq sat down behind her desk. "Close the door."

Galen did as instructed.

"Hawk Tasifa, you remember our conversation about keeping me informed?" Dove Haq asked. She sent a cold stare right through Prentice.

"I do..." Prentice said, taking in the fragments of the dove's accomplishments and adoration.

"It's been impossible to calm an egg in this situation. The entire community is wrapped in fear," Dove Haq interjected. "Add in the intense media scrutiny and the happiness is ripped away from campus. It has been all consuming, so for you to not keep me looped in..."

"Dove, we found the crown." Prentice held the item out to her. Her heart beat a little bit faster. "It's been recovered."

Dove Haq paused, mouth open in disbelief. Stunned, her lips moved, but nothing came out.

Prentice pressed the crown into the dove's hands and unwrapped it. Galen snickered from behind her. Prentice shot her a glare over her shoulder. Once Dove Haq's fingers wrapped around the crown, Prentice stepped back from her and returned to her position.

"Here's what we've done so far, Dove." Prentice nodded at Galen and they sat down in the chairs.

Dove Haq swallowed loud enough for them to hear. She was visibly emotional, as she turned to face them. She placed the crown on the desk and with trembling hands unwrapped it. The crown gleamed in the afternoon light.

"You found it." Dove Haq used the headwrap to touch it. She didn't put her fingers on it directly. "Where? Tell me everything."

Prentice nodded. "First, this is my condor, Galen."

Dove Haq said, "Hoot, Galen."

"Hoot, Dove." Galen raised her mechanical hand in greeting.

"As I first suspected, the crown's theft was an inside job." Prentice recounted what she and Galen learned and unearthed throughout their investigation.

When she finished, Prentice looked at Galen. "Did I miss anything?"

Galen shook her head. "No. That sums it up nicely."

Dove Haq listened and had only interrupted to ask clarifying questions. She sat, her eyes on the crown, her lips pressed together in concentration.

"Helena. All this time it had been her." Dove Haq shook her head as in disbelief. "And a wind user?"

"Yes." Prentice nodded. "I have seen this with my hawk eyes."

Dove Haq sighed and seemed shaken by what was unfolding. Her usual calm had been eroded and she shifted in her chair, her hands moving from the desk to her legs and back again. "This is horrible. You mentioned she was a dove in this nightjar group."

"Yes, though I don't blame the nightjars. They have long since practiced a different belief about the goddess, but Helena took advantage of them. She lacks empathy and has no loyalty. She dominated and manipulated everyone she came into contact with, Sebastian, Killion, and even Rook Renner."

"To what end? You said the theft wasn't financially motivated." Dove Haq across to Prentice.

"Power. She used the crown to strengthen the nightjars' faith in her as their leader," Prentice offered with a shrug. "Maybe the parishioners threatened to clip her wings."

"Perhaps she has a seared conscience," Galen said from behind Prentice.

"We didn't see the signs. Did anyone else have access to the crown at the chapel? You're sure she is the one who took it?" Dove Haq asked.

"She's troubled." Galen offered.

"I saw it with my own eyes, Killion stole the crown. Helena inflicted the damage to herself, to deflect suspicion, and to Pranske. She led Killion to believe she was a wind user and manipulated her into stealing the crown."

"By the goddess! We must capture her." Dove Haq stood up with a gleam in her eyes. "Do you know where these people lurk?"

"The eagles are searching for her," Galen said. "They're rotating search and recover teams throughout the egg and into the outer shell in a strategic grid search."

Dove Haq nodded. "And what of Killion's death? Any recent conflicts with someone? Her family is demanding answers, as are several students. What of the arson of the museum? I've been put in an intense situation. I must travel to Lanham to provide an account of the next steps and punishment for the culprit. Where are we with that?"

Prentice hesitated. "The two are connected. I suspect Helena had her hand in the museum fire and Killion's death. Perhaps Killion realized that she had been used and manipulated. Maybe Helena didn't want any more witnesses to the crown's theft."

Dove Haq raised an eyebrow. "Maybe?"

"We are still investigating," Prentice said. "We need to find Helena and interrogate her, Dove. Then we will get the answers we seek."

"Do you need any additional resources? I can call in the eagles from another egg as support," Dove Haq said. "I want this put to bed, Prentice."

Prentice couldn't agree more. "Yes, ma'am. We do have the crown, but there are loose ends that need tethering. I don't think we'll need additional resources, but I will let you know."

"Heed this. I want updates as you receive them." Dove Haq stood up, but she placed both hands on the desk, as if she needed support. "Do not continue to test me on this, Prentice."

The warning rang through to Prentice's heart. "Yes, ma'am."

"Oh, and Galen, do not think that you are exempt from my wrath," Dove Haq said, leaning slightly to make sure she caught Galen's good eye. "Your failure to check in with me will be noted in my report."

"Yes ma'am. My apologies, Dove," Galen bowed.

"I will keep you informed." Prentice started for the door.

"See that you do," Dove Haq said.

Galen left and Prentice started to leave as well.

"Prentice," Dove Haq said, her voice softened.

Prentice looked over her shoulder. "Yes, Dove?"

"Thank you."

"You're welcome, ma'am."

G alen and Prentice exited the building and stood outside in the afternoon heat. Students walked around the plaza and the campus grounds to class and the dining hall's delicious odors filled the area.

"That could've gone worse," Galen said, stretching toward the sun.

"I thought I told you to check in with her." Prentice shook her head. "Now you have a mark in your file."

"An ink mark is nothing compared to the marks on my body, Pren." Galen lifted her mechanical arm and moved it back and forth.

Prentice nodded. "Hoot."

"Hoot," Galen said. "Next steps."

"Just like I told the dove, I want to find Helena." Prentice reached into her utility belt and took out her tobacco rolled cigarettes. She lit the tip and smoked. "You haven't heard anything?"

"No," Galen said. She pulled out her bird caller. It remained blue. "No messages."

"Where would you go?" Prentice asked as she started toward the direction of her room.

"I would flee the egg," Galen said. "I put as much distance between myself and the chapel as possible."

Prentice paused. "I don't think she would. She wouldn't give up her power base and her followers. She's here. Did the eagles search the chapel?"

"Yes, and her residence as well as Sebastian's."

"Did you check Pranske's home?" Prentice asked.

"No, he's still in a coma," Galen said.

Prentice sighed. "We need to look there."

Galen nodded. "I'll call the eagles."

"No," Prentice touched her arm. "We need to go in quietly. She's a wind user, but I don't know how strong. If we send in an army of eagles, she'd respond in kind, out of fear. Let's see if we can talk her into giving herself up."

Galen shook her head and glared at Prentice with her one good eye. "When she doesn't, I'm going to cut her in half. Deal?"

Prentice inclined her head. "We need her alive."

"You'd be surprised what the body can live through," Galen said, turning away with a wave of her mechanical arm.

It gleamed in the sunlight.

P rentice removed her headwrap and sunk into the
bed's lumpy mattress. Over the last week, she'd
grown somewhat accustomed to the
uncomfortable bed. Still recovering from The Peacock
Ritual, Prentice's shoulders ached with fatigue. She needed
at least another twelve hours of rest. She'd sent Galen to
check out Pranske's home, but she wasn't to approach if
she found Helena. She trusted the condor to obey her, but
the decision didn't sit easy with Prentice. Galen was a
maverick and would fly off on her own when it suited her.
No amount of scolding, punishment, or red marks in her
file changed it.

Prentice massaged her scalp. She wanted to wash her
hair. The Sulidae dust, sand, and dryness did a number on
it, even with her hair wrap. She gave in and went to the
bathroom. She wouldn't be able to take bath, due to the
tiny, rectangular space, but she would be able to wash off
the day.

Once the water streams turned warm, Prentice stuck
her entire body beneath them. She lathered her hands with
her own soap she carried with her. There was a green bar
wrapped in tissue paper on the sink, but she preferred her
own. She had to get it shipped to her apartment in Lanham
from her home egg, Tsion. It included shea butter and salt
crystals from the Kahassi Sea. The soap scrubbed her
feathers and also rinsed cleaner than some of the other
soaps that left a film on her wings and her skin.

Prentice closed her eyes and moved the lather to her
hair. She took her time detangling her soft, locked hair, and
handling them beneath the rinse. With practiced breathing,

she blocked out the case, moving it to her subconscious as she worked on cleansing her body, her wings, and her mind.

She had a feeling in her feathers that she should treasure this time to recharge, to cleanse. Once they found Helena, and Prentice knew the eagles would locate her in Sulidae, things would get messy. Once she exited the shower, she'd get attuned with the case, but for now, she needed to rest and gain clarity.

As she ducked her head beneath the streams, she sighed. What lay ahead wouldn't be good, but she didn't want to admit it.

Not even to herself.

CHAPTER FOURTEEN

The *clop clop* of horses along the packed dirt streets reminded Prentice that despite the time of day, the Sulidae egg outside the university's campus went about its business. Color canopies and laughter filled the air as patrons covered in various dress, colorful headwraps, and hijabs that ranged from golden yellow to midnight black, went about their day. Scattered among them were more somber colored ghurtas. Daybreak unfolded in a peaceful manner, with an undercurrent of excitement to start the day.

Their open carriage allowed Prentice and Galen to enjoy the early morning coolness. The sun had crested the horizon and started its hike across the sky. It hadn't gotten too hot, for which Prentice was thankful. In the distance, a whistle blew, and a chapel's chimes announced the hour.

"Not too early for you," Galen said from beside Prentice.

"Not at all," Prentice said behind a yawn.

"Your hunch was right. It looks like someone is living in Pranske's home."

"Did the eagle get eyes on her?"

Galen shook her head. "But there's been some activity at the property. The sand across the porch has been disturbed. Witnesses reported seeing light in the rear back room, the one you can't see from the front."

"I see." Prentice rubbed her hands together.

Morning didn't sit well with her, but she wanted to put this to bed. Helena might not suspect them coming and they may be able to capture the wind user before she could engage her power. Prentice didn't want anyone hurt.

"She didn't see the eagles?" Prentice asked.

Galen shrugged. "I don't think so. I told them to wait and not to approach."

"And the witnesses? I don't want her to know we're coming."

Galen inclined her head. "I have done this work before, you know?"

Prentice smiled. "I know."

Their driver, a vulture, glanced at them over his shoulder, but remained silent. Prentice didn't want to spook Helena, and an eagle driver, large as they were, was difficult to hide. No, this would be best.

"Sebastian has been relocated to the birdcage?" Prentice pulled out her notepad and flipped through the pages.

"I collected him last evening. Quietly."

"Did he say anything?" Prentice looked over to Galen.

"He refused to speak." Galen's brows drew together. "It might be a minute before he feels like talking. Time in the birdcage loosens lips."

Prentice nodded. Sebastian had given them much

already. The rest would have to come from Helena and Pranske. If Pranske ever emerged from his induced coma.

"Dove Haq said they brought in an expert from Lanham," Prentice said to Galen. "Paige brought over a note and slipped it beneath my door early last evening."

"That's good," Galen said, with her gaze on the camels tethered outside an eatery. From the whiff of it, they sold carrion.

"She also included another reminder to keep her in the loop," Prentice said, holding her nose as their carriage passed. "Have you eaten?"

Galen turned to her, the damaged eye moving in concert with its mate. "Yes. Last evening, but that place had some fresh. I could smell it. Once this is over, I'm coming back."

Prentice laughed. "Sure thing. You understand if I won't join you."

"We're flockmates. I get it."

Prentice sat up straight in her seat as the landscape melded into one of a hushed quiet. Nightjars slept during the day, and once the carriage crossed into the Nightendale neighborhood the Sulidae bustle dwindled to a hush. Every now and again the beating wings of insects or the love call of crickets could be heard.

She scanned the buildings as they passed the now open street. As the only carriage, they had the road to themselves aside from a few individuals on camels. How many watched from behind closed doors and slivers of shaded windows? Prentice inched forward in her seat.

"Quiet."

"Too quiet." Galen flexed her mechanical fingers and checked her sheathed sword. "I feel like we're walking into a trap."

Prentice's suspicions heightened.

Sure, it was quiet, but an undercurrent made the air tense. It held a grittiness that got in her mouth. Prentice's adrenaline was going. Despite the planned surprise, she had the worst feeling in her stomach, but shoved it aside. The silence felt so terrible.

The crown's recovery set fire to the case, but if they didn't find Helena it would become an ember. Prentice needed to resolve it. Her options were dwindling. Nothing else mattered at this point.

As they approached Pranske's multifamily home, Prentice's feathers rose. The dwelling sat seemingly deserted with a stack of bicycles casually leaning against the building's front. The rectangular windows, narrow and dark, appeared as a wincing tan face. No porch. She slowed and gestured for Galan to go around the other side. Behind them three eagles, dressed in taupe one-piece uniforms flanked out as well. Two followed Prentice and the other one walked behind Galen.

Pranske shared his home with his sister, brother, and their families, but the eagles' intelligence provided information about a secluded structure in the back. Detached from the home, it served as a garden house or mother-in-law's home. A bit too obvious, but then Helena's folly had been in her thinking she had outsmarted everyone.

Galan came from the other side, Prentice's right. They reached the door, and Prentice raised her hand, counting down from five, silently with just her fingers.

The closer they came to the door, the wind grew stronger. The eagles pulled their masks pulled over their noses. Prentice squinted against the blowing sand. It hit her cheeks, but she kept her face pointed toward her objective—the front door.

She waved the two eagles ahead. They approached with batons kept close to their torsos. Once they reached the door, they flanked on either side. They proceeded to barge in, sending the door splintering off its hinges. They rushed in like a tornado of shouts and physical domination.

Prentice followed, her own talons drawn at the ready. The one room sat in dusky shadow. Her eyes adjusted as furniture, a large area rug, pots filled with plants came into view.

"Hoot, Helena." Prentice greeted the woman seated to her right with her back against the wall. This room housed mostly plants, tools, and instruments to grow, use, and preserve plants and their fruit. Beneath that earthiness lurked a foul odor that she recognized as decomposing flesh.

"Get. Up!" Galen ordered as she entered, sword in hand, face set to slay. The door creaked announcing her entry.

The five of them made a semi-circle around her. She looked up at them with wide, angry eyes. The lantern at her feet cast a small circle around her.

"This is over," Prentice said.

Prentice met Helena's hardened gaze and a cold pit dropped into her stomach. There was nothing behind her eyes. She had large, empty eyes, like they were dead. It clicked then. What was the wedge between the three of them? Killion. She put herself between the triangle of best friends.

Helena underestimated how much Prentice knew.

Prentice removed both talons. "Be on guard for wind magic."

"You know of wind magic. Of course, you know. Hawks see the unseen, even the invisible, I suppose." Helena got to her feet.

The eagles shifted like a movable wall as she did so.

"Let's go outside," Helena said.

Prentice nodded. Galen shook her head in warning, but she knew the risk of a wind user outside with free access to the wind. Dangerous, but she wanted a confession. Galen made her way to Prentice's side.

Galen leaned over to Prentice. "She's trying to negotiate the situation to her benefit."

Prentice kept her eyes ahead. "I'm aware."

Galen grunted at her.

"It's been very emotional for Killion's family, Helena," Prentice said to Helena as they stopped just outside the single room building.

"It wasn't supposed to be like this. It all deteriorated," Helena said.

"You had malice and forethought," Galen said. She kept her sword pointed at Helena.

"The truth is the truth," Prentice said. "That's all I'm seeking."

Despite Helena's forced calm, Prentice saw the rage was there. She needed to delve deeper. Her heart leapt as Helena's shoulders slacked.

"This is a big day," Galen said.

"As long as we get corroborating evidence," Prentice said loud enough for only Galen to hear.

"You're not always who your family thinks you are," Prentice said to Helena.

"Wouldn't you do anything for your crew?" Helena kept her hands pressed together pointed downward.

The wind ruffled her bangs and the fabric of her green headdress. Prentice's hands tightened around her talons. Would Helena come quietly or cause a ruckus as the roosters say? She needed to keep her calm.

"You lash out at Pranske because of a triangle or was he a spurned lover threatening you? Was the attack in the heat of the moment?" Prentice watched for her reaction.

Helena shrugged and avoided eye contact. Her body language conveyed she wasn't telling the truth, but none of Prentice's theories provoked a response.

Galen's hand tightened around her sword's hilt.

Helena looked up. "Pranske held an angry view of women not fully nightjars."

Prentice's heart sank. She wanted truth, not spin.

"Like you."

"Yeah, but I grew in power. The goddess spoke to me."

"Then came Killion."

"Yes." Helena sighed.

"All of the fantasies evaporated when Killion crashed into your trio, but she threatened your status. Was she pushing the parishioner to pay more?"

"Everyone gravitated to her," Helena said, her brow crinkled. "She tried to steal my power. That is unforgivable."

"Unforgiveable." Prentice shook her head. "That is one of the goddess's pillars."

Helena glared. "I'll admit, Hawk, I was hurt, angry..."

"Jealous," Prentice interjected.

"No." Helena hitched her chin up.

Those toxic elements combined drove Helena to do all

she'd done, but at its core, it was all about greed. It contorted and changed everything in its path. Evil had been in their presence and they didn't know it.

"A false prophet should have his face destroyed!" Helena shouted.

"These are ravings." Galen raised her sword over her head.

Prentice kept her calm.

"How could she take something the goddess bestowed?" Prentice asked. The notion was absurd. Surely, Helena saw that.

Helena stiffened, drawing her hands up to her chest. Prentice's remark sobered her.

"Killion deserved it. If she was truly the goddess's anointed, she would've rose from the flames." Helena smirked.

"You knew she wouldn't when you struck the match," Prentice said. "She had knowledge she shared with students, with parishioners, and you snuffed it out."

"Knowledge is a dangerous word, Hawk."

"Let's go, Helena. This is done," Prentice gestured with one left hand. "Come on."

"No." With that she muttered an incantation.

The gust swept through them. She fell onto the hard-packed earth, but Prentice expected it. Instead of fighting the blow, she tumbled with it, tucking her talon close as she did so. *Magic takes focus.* Unfortunately for Helena, she had four other targets that snared her attention. She took her gaze off of Prentice.

She righted herself, she aimed and fired. There was a cold feeling when she had to shoot someone she didn't know.

The blue tendrils curled from Prentice's talon clutched in her right hand. "What's this? Failure to launch another escape plan?" Prentice asked Helena.

Galen rushed to secure Helena, pulling a cloth scarf around her mouth to gag her. She said to Prentice, "That was fast."

"I couldn't risk any more lives," Prentice said.

The winds rumbling gave it away. Even now, the tingling lingered on the wind, like bitter aftertaste of Helena's disappointment.

"Seems anticlimactic," Galen said. "I wanted a fight."

Prentice smirked as she put her talon away. "You wanted violence."

Galen snatched Helena up from the ground. Helena struggled, but Galen had been secured her hands behind her. The eagles closed and moved together as a walled unit toward the carriages. The breeze rustled their clothes.

"None of us are free from weakness," Galen said to Prentice.

CHAPTER FIFTEEN

THREE DAYS LATER

The next three days unfolded in a blur of sleeping, eating, and writing her report for The Order. Prentice found herself outside the rental room for the first time in those three days. She'd had food ordered in, Galen dropped them off and the cleaner came in and took care of the apartment.

Now, standing in the medical center, Prentice watched the doctor check Pranske's vital signs. Dove Haq had been briefed. The reporters had fallen away and life on campus returned to normal. Well, what accounted for normal in Sulidae.

Pranske sat up like a statue, but his breathing was strained. Located in the drab corner of the room, his thin bed and thick blankets consumed most of the space. Dark, red eyes peered across his bed's expanse at Prentice, who stood with pad and pencil in hand. Beneath the lavender odor of healing earth magic laid the faint odor of rotting, stinking flesh.

"Are you managing okay?" Prentice arched an eyebrow and glanced at the doctor for an answer.

"Yeah." Pranske wheezed.

"Will he need to go back under?" Prentice shifted her weight to her other foot.

The doctor said, "The Order gets what they demand. We brought him out of the coma earlier than recommended."

"I'm sitting right here!" Pranske held out his arms. "Why would Helena do this?"

Prentice shrugged. "Jealousy makes people do strange things, but you knew it was Helena and not Killion."

He nodded and as he lowered his arms, tears welled. "Magic is bestowed by the goddess. She wasn't one of us. Everybody knows ostriches can't magic."

"Then Helena goes berserk if anyone threatened her fragile hold on the chapel," Pranske added.

"And you? What about your threats to Killion?"

"She was using him. He's my brother. I couldn't let that go," Pranske said.

"That's why you didn't warn her about Helena." Prentice raised an eyebrow.

Pranske fell back into the pillows propped up behind him.

"Your silence got her killed."

Pranske shook his head. "No. She brought it on herself."

"One last question. Why follow her leadership?" Prentice asked.

Pranske closed his eyes. "I followed the true Ocho. I love the goddess. I trusted her to sort it."

"And that cost you both your hands." Prentice remarked, nodding at his bandage wrists.

Pranske didn't answer or open his eyes. "Leave me."

"You knew how devious Helena could be. Yet, you did nothing."

He sighed. "When we were fledglings, she kept herself to herself, and her thoughts too. In the last four turns, she became more vocal at sessions. In like a blink, the goddess spoke to her and boom, she's the Ocho."

"And working as a guard at the museum." Prentice looked across to him. "You didn't know anything about the theft?"

"No. Recently, I'd been keeping my distance from her, except at work. Cracks were already beginning to show between the ostrich and her."

Prentice shook her head slowly in disbelief at Pranske's gall. "Why did she take your hands?"

He winced. He dropped his gaze as tears spilled over and coursed down his cheeks. "I told you. I dunno."

"The hands tell all kinds of stories. What tale did Helena want to keep yours from telling?"

"I know it isn't tumbling out of me like you want. I'm tired. Exhausted and hungry." He rubbed his forearm against the dark new growth along his jawline.

"Hawk Tasifa." The doctor gave her a warning glare.

"Hoot," Prentice said in acknowledgement. Then to Pranske, "You know, you either stole something, hit her, or..."

"Jealousy, as you mentioned before," Sebastian said as

he entered the room. He stopped short, looked at Pranske, and then Prentice. "He is an amazing gardener. She'd always envied his ability to create and grow living things. It carried favor with members of our chapel, and she didn't like it."

"She took his hands so he couldn't garden." Prentice couldn't believe it. The reasoning seemed so petty.

"Hoot, friend," Sebastian said to Pranske and went up to sit beside him opposite the doctor. "I thought you were done with us."

"Wrapping up loose ends." Prentice closed the notepad. She'd never get the real reason Helena took Pranske's hands.

"A word, Hawk Tasifa?" Rook Renner stood at the threshold behind Sebastian.

"We were done." Prentice put her items away. "Sebastian, Pranske, The Order will be in contact around witnessing and coming down to the judgments. May the goddess guide you."

With that she walked out with rook. He stroked his beard as he spoke.

"I owe you thanks for getting to the bottom of this unpleasantness," Rook Renner said. "I overheard Sebastian and a bit from Pranny. That's not the Helena I know."

"We all have our baggage we keep locked in dark closets," Prentice said.

"Yes."

"Investigations take various twists and turns," Prentice said.

"I'm certain." Rook Renner gave her a rare smile.

"What happens to the museum? The artifacts?" Prentice asked.

Rook Renner sighed. "It will be rebuilt, with better security. The crown, I heard, had been returned."

"Yes. Where is it now?"

"The Order sent a set of condors to take it back to Lanham. It's back there under a heavier lock and key. I doubt we'll see the crown on display again." He tugged on his beard. "No, I don't think we will."

They walked downstairs and out into the bright, sunny day. Cooler than recent days, the breezes smelled of yuccas and desert blossoms.

Prentice turned to him. "It was great to see you again."

Rook Renner inclined his head. "You've turned out to be an intelligent and fine hawk, Prentice."

"Thank you." Prentice blushed. It was high praise form a rook.

"When do you leave?" he asked as they started walking again.

"Tomorrow, early morning." Prentice answered.

"Got a new assignment?" Rook Renner held up a gold envelope.

Even cupped in his hand, she still spied The Order's seal. "I'm guessing my answer should be yes."

The rook smiled. "It came to the dove's office, and she asked me to pass it on to you. She had to leave earlier this morning—a conference in Lanham."

"Of course." Prentice took the envelope. "Thank you."

"Well, this is goodbye," Rook Renner said. "May the goddess guide you, Hawk Tasifa."

"May she also reside with you, Rook Renner." Prentice bowed again.

Prentice watched the rook walk away, his robes billowing around his ankles, making it look like he floated, but she saw his sandals remained on the ground. She had no doubt he'd get the goddess museum back up and running, better than ever. When one almost loses their most important object, they'd do anything to keep it—and they tended to cherish it. Helena proved that point.

She returned to the rental room, turned the key, and entered. Her travel bags remained opened where she had begun packing for her next trip. The table had Prentice's copious notes scattered all over its scarred surface. Last night's empty sweet milk bottle sat amongst the parchments.

Her mind turned to Helena as it had the last few days. Galen left to escort the former Ocho to be detained by the court in Lanham. The large, magically secure birdcage resided just outside of Lanham, in the outer shell, a multi-floor building with windowless rooms. Mages kept it secure in coordination with condor guards.

Killion's death had been a heinous and cold-blooded act. Helena's resentment had grown deeper despite the friendship mask she wore. That betrayal hinted at a deeper malice in sweet-faced Helena. Prentice tried to interview her again, but she only spoke in ramblings.

Had the goddess spoken to Helena and driven her mad?

The duality became her burden. Helena allowed fear into her thoughts. She'd been taunting, cruel, and a sinister temperament enhanced by fear. None of those qualities were embraced by the goddess.

That fear fed Helena's greed for power and jealousy. The chapel allowed her to feel important, thus reinforcing her delusions. She lashed out as it crumbled down around her. As she soared in the chapel's ranks, she lost sight of the goddess's face, and fell. Hard.

Prentice sat down on the bed. She couldn't help but think about the curse on those who touched the crown. Killion did and she died in a fiery death. Helena touched it also and she burnt up her status, her life, too. Could a kernel of truth reside in those warnings?

She dug out her remaining tobacco and rolled it into a slender cigarette. Once she lit it, Prentice sat cross-legged on the bed and smoked. She emptied her mind of everything that occurred the last week. Like a sieve, it to poured out of her. Mentally, she had to prepare for the next assignment.

At this, she glanced over to the golden envelope on the table. The Order's insignia rose from the blue wax that sealed the parchment together.

It can wait.

CHAPTER SIXTEEN

A rare summer squall rained down on Sulidae as Prentice awaited the vulture and his covered carriage to take her to the train station. Galen held the umbrella that kept them both from getting drenched.

"Where are you headed next?" Galen asked.

"I'm not sure."

Galen turned to her. "No new assignment? After what we did here? The court is gonna give you a vacation. That seems unlike them."

"I didn't say *that*." Prentice smiled.

"Maybe we'll get assigned together." Galen turned her gaze ahead at the pouring rain.

The approaching carriage's covered lanterns lights glowed in the gray gloom.

"Look, there's my ride," Prentice said.

Galen cleared her throat. "We make a good team. Always have."

Prentice adjusted her headwrap. "I will have a commendation placed in your file."

"Pren..." Galen's metal hand grabbed her shoulder. "I..."

"Hoot! You going to the train station?" the vulture driver shouted down to her. He wore a dark cloak with a hood that cast his gray skinned face into shadow. Only the gleaming of his dark eyes could be seen.

"Hoot, yes!" Prentice answered, thankful for the interruption.

The driver took her luggage bags and placed them on the back of the carriage, securing them with leather straps. He then covered them with a tarp. Prentice watched this and when he opened the door, she turned to Galen.

At university she and Galen bonded over long walks and pots of coffee as Lanham had some of the richest coffee fields in the kingdom. Over time their relationship became contentious until Galen left for training.

Then nothing. No letters. No visits.

Only the remaining grief that ran deep and a vulnerable Prentice.

It still hurt.

"It's been good to see you, Galen. Goodbye." Prentice pulled her into a brief hug before releasing her.

Without another word, she climbed into the carriage and slammed the door with her heart in her throat.

"Damn you, Pren!" Galen shouted as the carriage pulled away from the university.

The rain drowned out the rest of her words.

The tightness in Prentice's throat eased the farther away from Galen and the university they traveled. The carriage's dark interior comforted her. For once, she didn't want to see anything. She closed her eyes, but the envelope in her cloak's pocket tugged at her conscience.

With the nagging ruffling her feathers, she snapped her fingers, sparking a small flame. It provided enough illumination to read the envelope's message.

"Surely I am due a rest." Prentice grumbled to no one in particular.

Prentice used her pen dagger to slice open the sealed letter. She wanted it to go home.

Hawk Tasifa—

Congratulations on your success in Sulidae and the recovery of the Five Feathered Crown. You are truly favored by the goddess. It is for this reason the next assignment must be in person, but first rest.

Please return to Lanham. We are extending a brief reprieve; however, you are to meet with me within one week from today. There is an assignment I would like to discuss with you.

Speak of this to no one until we have met.

The truth is light.

Peace,
Cardinal Wick

Prentice used her left hand to fold the letter and replaced it into the envelope. She turned the golden paper over and took in the wax seal. It came from The Order. Although happy to not have to bounce right to another assignment, Cardinal Wick's wording hinted at something troubling. Prentice wondered about how The Order had handled the crown's theft, and perhaps heads had rolled.

She wondered who had been kicked out of the proverbial nest and sent sailing from the lofty branches of court.

"Ma'am, we've arrived." The driver wrenched open the door and snatched down the steps.

"Thank you," Prentice said as she stepped out into the now cloudy day.

The rain had stopped.

But Prentice knew that it was only a calm before the storm.

She adjusted her cloak, her talons, and took up her luggage bags.

Come what may, she would discover it as she'd always done.

See the unseen.

THE END

Love it? Hate it? Drop us a review.

ABOUT NICOLE GIVENS KURTZ

Nicole Givens Kurtz is an author, editor, and educator. She's the recipient of the Horror Writers Association's Diversity Grant (2020). She's been named as one of Book Riot's Best Black Indie SFF Writers. She's also the editor of the groundbreaking anthology, SLAY: Stories of the Vampire Noire. Her novels have been a finalist in the Dream Realm Awards, Fresh Voices, and EPPIE Awards for science fiction. She's written for White Wolf, Bram Stoker Finalist in Horror Anthology, Sycorax's Daughters, and Serial Box's The Vela: Salvation series. Nicole has over 40 short stories published as well as 11 novels and three active speculative mystery series. She's a member of Horror Writers Association, Sisters in Crime, and Science Fiction Writers of America. You can support her work via Patreon and find more about her at http://www.nicolegivenskurtz.net.

NICOLE'S WHEREABOUTS ON THE WEB:

Other Worlds Pulp-http://www.nicolegivenskurtz.net

Join Nicole Givens Kurtz's Newsletter-http://www.nicolegivenskurtz.net/newsletter

Follow Nicole on Twitter-@nicolegkurtz

Follow on Facebook-http://www.facebook.com/nicolegkurtz

facebook.com/nicolegkurtz
twitter.com/nicolegkurtz

The First Kingdom of Aves Mystery

The Cybil Lewis Science Fiction Mystery Series

The Soul Cages: A Minister Knight of Souls Novel

Made in the USA
Columbia, SC
25 October 2022

70017877R00107